LAVENDER NICOLE

Tattooed on Their Hearts

Copyright © 2024 by Lavender Nicole

All rights reserved. No part of this publication may be reproduced, stored or transmitted in any form or by any means, electronic, mechanical, photocopying, recording, scanning, or otherwise without written permission from the publisher. It is illegal to copy this book, post it to a website, or distribute it by any other means without permission.

First edition

This book was professionally typeset on Reedsy. Find out more at reedsy.com

*To those who wanna be sluts, but their trauma makes it difficult.
Let your inner slut out, even if it's just while you're reading.*

Contents

Introduction	1
Prologue	3
Chapter 1	6
Chapter 2	12
Chapter 3	16
Chapter 4	20
Chapter 5	23
Chapter 6	27
Chapter 7	28
Chapter 8	34
Chapter 9	36
Chapter 10	41
Chapter 11	45
Chapter 12	49
Chapter 13	52
Chapter 14	57
Chapter 15	62
Chapter 16	67
Chapter 17	72
Chapter 18	77
Chapter 19	84
Chapter 20	86
Chapter 21	87
Chapter 22	92

Chapter 23	95
Chapter 24	98
Chapter 25	102
Chapter 26	105
Chapter 27	112
Chapter 28	117
Chapter 29	123
Chapter 30	126
Chapter 31	128
Chapter 32	131
Chapter 33	141
Chapter 34	145
Chapter 35	149
Chapter 36	158
Chapter 37	162
Chapter 38	167
Chapter 39	172
Chapter 40	179
Chapter 41	182
Acknowledgments	190
About the Author	191

Introduction

Trigger Warnings: Grief, suicide, emotional abuse, PTSD, FFM sexual interactions, SA mentions, pregnancy, and kinks like breeding. This book contains sensitive matters that may be hard to read. This is someone growing from witnessing their partner's suicide. I wanted anyone like me to have a love story where the widow(er) heals and finds love. You are not alone. You can keep going and find someone (or several someones) to be there for you. Your mental health is important, so if this book could trigger you please be careful. You are loved. You have this. You are not alone.

Please note while some of this does come from my personal history, not all of it does. I have taken experiences I have read about and talked to other widows about and combined them. This story has aspects that are very true to many relationships that end in suicide, so if that is triggering for you please do not read this book. Your mental health matters. If you are a widow or widower and ever need someone to talk to, I am here. I hope this book makes you feel seen. I rarely feel seen in the books I read, because most people don't think of widows/widowers as young adults. Never in my life did I imagine I would be a widow in my 30's, but here we are. My goal with this book was to open people's eyes to the truth many people face. Personally my PTSD does tend to hold me back. My goal is to release this book in October to have an impact on my own narrative. I want to change October from the month I witnessed my husband's suicide to the month I released my debut novel. I wanted to be inclusive in this book, if you feel I wrote anyone in an aspect that is done poorly please let me know. I love y'all and thank you for supporting me on this journey.

Here is a spotify link to a short playlist for the book! https://open.spotify.com/playlist/3kT5gMKXzbSe0vou9O6Gv8?si=ag2gGcgwRMColBgK9vSRGQ&pi=Bxp5klUHSc2JW

This book is fiction and is not meant to educate anyone on bdsm/kink. Please do research and stay safe. Kinks include -but not limited to- praise, degradation, breeding, exhibition, voyeur, and light impact.

Prologue

River

Therapy had always been hard for me and I was never consistent with it, but with my PTSD and flashbacks, I decided I needed to stick to it. Dr. Alex had a way about her that just made me comfortable and feel like I was talking to a friend. It was such a safe space, and after years of feeling like I was walking a tightrope while holding expensive, breakable objects, I needed that. I needed to feel like the words and emotions that left my mouth were not going to cause someone to scream in my face. I needed to know that my words mattered; my emotions mattered; that I deserved to be able to talk about my feelings.

Therapy has brought so much peace into my life. I was relaxing back on the comfortable black couch, holding the soft, fuzzy, pale blue throw pillow to my chest, and looking out of the window. Zoning out, my mouth seemed to just start moving. "I used to love the rain, the comforting pitter patter hitting the roof. No bright sun; beautiful clouds. It relaxed me, but now...." I trailed off and blinked the tears away. It took me a moment to continue, and Dr. Alex waited, no pressure, just support. "But now, the rain drops mimic the splatter of blood. Sometimes...sometimes, when the rain hits just right, it sounds like a gunshot."

The rain had my memories from that torturous night close to the surface, it may have been a little over two years but time passed differently now. As I stared at the rain, washing the day off my shitty Jeep, I was transported back to that night. The memories vividly replayed in my vision, causing me to relive the night from hell. I let the tears fall as I fell deeper into my memories.

The rain was beating down on the hood of my old, decrepit Jeep, the splashing water continuing to mimic the blood splatter in my flashback. I finally started speaking, telling Dr. A about the night. "I was numb as I stared blankly out the window, waiting for the police to show up. 6 minutes. It took them 6 minutes to get to me after I told them he had a gun. Even after I told them I was worried for my own life. It still took 6 minutes. Once they arrived, the flood gates opened again. I was bawling and hyperventilating; scared. They were gonna ask questions. What if they thought I did it? What if they thought I murdered him and his suicide took even more from my life? Was it going to take my freedom too? Shortly after the police arrived, an officer approached me. He was a stout, balding, white man; the guy you picture as a cop. I think he said his name was John, but I truly do not know or care. I don't remember much about our conversation. He offered me a priest, I said no, and then the real conversation started."

I stopped for a moment, taking a deep breath before continuing on with my story. "The officer asked me what happened. It took me a few seconds to respond, to find the words. Finally, I started talking. I couldn't look him in the eyes, so I stared blankly over his shoulder. I started by telling him about our fight. I couldn't find the words, so I was blunt and said "We got into a fight. It was awful. He was screaming in my face and called me a 'terminal illness'." I had to take a breath before I could continue. "The words terminal illness taunt me daily." I turned away, giving myself permission to cry and took a few deep breaths.

After breathing deeply, I was able to continue. "I explicitly remember what I said to the cop, and it was an apology. I witnessed his suicide and I apologized?!" My outrage over that seemed to be more today. "Why did I feel the need to apologize? I remember saying, 'That's when he pulled the revolver and I immediately called y'all. I am so sorry y'all have to see what I saw; no one needs to see that.' From there, I sat in my Jeep outside the shop and waited for the cops to be finished. I waited for my support system to come and waited for his Dad, with all the drama that came with him. I waited, hoping for the entire thing to be over. But it will never be over." I turned back to my therapist after my story and gave her a small, sad smile. "It's been about a month and I can still hear my own screams anytime it's quiet." Dr. Alex, a beautiful black woman with curves for days, eventually asked me, "Who was your support system? And do not say your dogs, even though I know they have been a huge comfort to you." I chuckled a moment; my dogs are a huge part of my support system. I thought for a minute and finally responded, "My best friend Fe has been instrumental in all of this, and his husband too. But my parents have also been my rocks. The fact that they let me and the dogs move home so I wouldn't be alone, has been such a relief." Dr. A and I talked for another 30 minutes, then I drove home listening to the "Zodiac Academy" series for the hundredth time, finding comfort in the characters.

Chapter 1

Zane

Tattoos could sometimes be so frustrating to design. The client I had coming in later today wanted a common tattoo, one of those half lion head tattoos, but I was determined to make it unique. I prided myself on how I make tattoos personal, but for some reason this one had me stumped. Probably because I didn't know much about this client and all I could think about was a "dude bro" vibe. How should I individualize this typical "dude bro" tattoo? Sighing, I laid my iPad down on the counter, rubbing my temples in frustration.

Just then, one of the most beautiful people I had ever laid eyes on, walked through the door. I was suddenly glad the counter was blocking my bottom half; insta-boners aren't the most professional thing in the world and I could tell this client was someone I was going to want to work with. She had a soft belly that made me want to lay my head on it while cuddling, and thighs that were on full display; pale with some small tattoos and cellulite. The curves on this woman! She wore a short, deep plum colored dress with long sleeves, and a V-neck that gave a hint of generous cleavage. It flowed around her as if she was trying to hide herself, but when it hit just right, I was rewarded with the outline of her Rubenesque form. Her image had my

CHAPTER 1

mouth watering and my cock twitched in excitement. There was a cloud of sadness and strength that surrounded her, and I immediately wanted to know more. Her eyes drew me in; the feeling as if my soul was being pulled to hers. The energy that surrounded her was a beacon to mine, like it was calling for something missing.

When she walked up to the counter and spoke, her silky voice was like a siren's call luring me in. "Hey." With that single word she somehow managed to sound powerful, yet unsure. I was captivated and gave her a small smile. "How can I help you?" With a shy smile back she said, "I'm River. I was hoping to get a piece done." River, I liked that. Her name seemed to fit her well. "Zane. I'm one of the owners here at Vivid Ink. What are you looking to get done?"

I was enthralled; her voice, her curves, her presence in general was so captivating. The way River seemed to radiate gentleness and strength. Everything about her drew me in. Her eyes were a deep azure, reminding me of an ocean at once, both peaceful and mysterious. It felt as if her soul was speaking to me through them. I had no idea how I knew, but I felt it deep within me that something traumatizing had happened to this beautiful woman. A sudden, overwhelming feeling of possessiveness and protectiveness flooded my system, shocking me, because I had only ever felt like that with Raven. I still couldn't get over how much I liked her name, River. Rivers tended to be powerful, strong, beautiful, and wild and something about her presence made me feel she also exhibited those traits.

"I have an idea about a tattoo. Do you have a portfolio I could look at?" When she blinked at me and tilted her head, it became clear that she was waiting on a response. "Yes, I can grab mine, that way you can see if my art style is a good fit for you." A huge smile took over her face and she nodded. I moved around the counter, pulling my portfolio out to show her.

We sat next to each other on one of the cozy, midnight blue couches in our lobby. Around us, our bare cement walls were covered in various drawings done by myself and some of our other artists. The couches surrounded an oval glass table, whose white legs echoed that of a sandy beach, lending to a calm environment. I passed her the navy blue album with *Zane* painted on it. She flipped through it, occasionally stopping and running her hands across various images. I loved watching her long delicate fingers caress my art; it felt like she was touching a piece of me.

She bit her lip and her eyes darted away like she was nervous. I was already so captivated with this beautiful goddess, it scared me. But fuck it. I wasn't one to do things by halves, I was gonna embrace the feelings and follow my heart.

"A few months ago..." she trailed off. Her eyes filled with some dark memory from her past.

I waited, immediately wanting more information, but not wanting to push her. I got the feeling rushing her to talk about what she wanted and needed, would backfire spectacularly for me.

With a deep breath she continued. "A few months ago, I was a close witness to a violent act by gun." Her voice caught, and in that moment I felt like her pain was mine. "I won't go into all the details yet, but I want a tattoo that shows how much stronger I have become on the other side of the experience. I think I'd like some flowers blooming through ash, with pawprints of three dogs within the ash. Maybe some flames in the background. But I'm not the artist, you are." She pulled up her shorts to show her thick thighs. I noticed she had

CHAPTER 1

freckles and dimples splayed on the canvas of her pale skin. "I was thinking the front of my left thigh would be a good place for it. What do you think, Zane?"

My brain immediately started working through design options. I couldn't wait to feel my tattoo needle vibrating as my other hand gripped her shapely thigh. I could already imagine the small sounds of pain she might make as I marked her. I wasn't usually one to have the alpha *"mine"* brain, but damn! I felt like banging my chest while yelling *"mine"*, like some sort of tattoo shop Tarzan.

I couldn't help but think that this tattoo would help pull me out of my creative slump. This wasn't one of the typical "dude bro" tattoos. This was personal. It truly meant something. Don't get me wrong, lions make beautiful tattoos and can have a lot of meaning, but something about this tattoo design just felt so right. Like fate knew this was a tattoo I needed to be a part of.

I was stunned, excited, and honestly a little taken aback in the best possible way. One of the reasons I loved my job was that I got to help people heal through art, my art. I helped clients express themselves. Or sometimes I just got to give someone a dumb or fun tattoo and have a great time. I was sure my excitement was going to be clear in my answer. "I love this idea and would be honored if you'd let me design it for you. How much were you looking to spend and what's your time frame? Also, what pronouns do you use? Sorry, I should have asked previously. I use He/Him."

When River finally responded, my eyes jumped back to hers. I kept catching myself skimming her curves with my eyes. "She/Her/Hers. I appreciate you asking. I'd like to get it done as soon as possible and the max I have is $900. Will that be enough for this? I know it's a lot of work and detail?"

River was messing with her hair and randomly chewing on her bottom lip. Watching her wear those full, pouty lips had me wanting to go over there and bite them, as if they were mine to bite and do with as I pleased. It was clear to me that River was nervously waiting for my answer. I hoped she was excited too. "I can certainly do that for about $900. You seem to radiate bright colors and a vibrant personality. With the multiple shades of purple in your hair and various neon french tips on your nails, is it safe to assume you would like color in your tattoo?"

She chuckled softly. "I was thinking a little gloom with bright colors popping through it? It speaks to my vibrancy fighting through the darkness that has tried to over take my life."

When we finally got all the details discussed, set a date, and I took her deposit, she exited the shop. I immediately got to designing her tattoo. I knew I was falling prey to my whims by starting on her design and not finishing the ones I already started, but fuck it.

Taking a break from River's tattoo, I finished the lion. He had a beautiful mane with a stormy background. Clouds, a forceful wind, and a dark palette combined to portray an obvious storm. When my client Trey saw it, he was thrilled. It spoke to him and we got started. After 5 hours, where Trey continuously complained about the pain, we were finally finished. Trey went on his way, and I could let my mind obsess over River's tattoo.

The next day, I was looking at the design and trying to figure out what was missing. I had finished my last client about two hours ago and had been working on River's design ever since.

CHAPTER 1

Overall, it turned out to be a good day. I decided that I needed to take a break from looking at River's tattoo and come back to it with a new perspective. I closed my eyes and focused on the sounds and feel of my surroundings. The shop always had a variety of 2000's music playing; what could I say, we were nostalgic millennials. Mixed in with the music was the random jingle of the automatic bell above the door and the soft hum of tattooing needles. We had taken multiple deposits for tattoos today and Raven had several walk-in piercings. A decent day all around, but River's tattoo still had me stuck. It had been a while since I had a tattoo that challenged me in such a meaningful way. I wanted to make sure it was perfect for her. The design was speaking to me, I just couldn't figure out what it was trying to say. Knowing the history that brought her in for this tattoo made it all the more important to make sure I got it just right. Just as I was getting ready to tackle the project again, I felt familiar fingers graze my shoulders and I knew my evening was about to become a lot more exciting.

Chapter 2

Raven

As I entered our shop through the back door, from grabbing a fast lunch, and walked down the dimly lit blue hall, I stopped in Zane's tattoo room. It was a light gray color with beautiful vivid art absolutely everywhere. I just stopped and stared for a minute. Zane was truly something to look at. His light brown skin with slight freckles and short, black, curly hair always grabbed my attention. I could tell he was hard at work and zoned into his art, so I walked up behind him and ran my fingers across his back. I could feel the tension leave his shoulders as he relaxed into my touch. Zane and I hadn't always had a great relationship; we were best friends with benefits *before* our parents got together. When our parents announced their relationship, it brought a lot of tension into ours. We prevailed, however, and now our love had grown into so much more. We were able to find comfort in each other, and grew stronger through it all. Our connection blossomed and we became even more than we had been before. If anything, the turbulence our parents brought into our relationship ended up bringing us strength and stability together. In addition, our love of art and color had always connected us, and we used that to communicate and grow together. Ultimately, this growth led

CHAPTER 2

us to opening up our shop, Vivid Ink.

I knew whatever art he was working on was important to him. He put time and effort into all his art, but he only ever got this worked up when it was something truly special. I peeked over his shoulder to see a background of ash with three different sized paw prints walking through it and random bursts of color in the forms of bright blooming flowers. It was truly beautiful and I immediately wanted to know the story behind it.

When he turned in his chair to look up, I knew he needed me. The look in his eyes had me dropping to my knees in front of him. We both loved the risk of getting caught, especially by our employees while in our shop. We had learned the love of the risk when we were teens sneaking around, trying to hide our relationship from my parents. Though, when we did get caught, it was awkward. I shook my head to rid myself of the thoughts of the past and concentrate on right now.

The chance of being caught had already left my dark blue cotton thong soaked. I knew I shut the door, but I certainly did not lock it, and that knowledge spurred on the feelings of excitement and desire. I knew it was risky, and probably stupid, but at the moment I did not care. Zane wouldn't care either. From my knees, I was going to bring my beautiful man as much stress relief and pleasure as I could. I sensually crawled under his desk, feeling his eyes burning into my back. Watching me like a predator watching their prey, his gaze made me feel like a goddess. Hidden from prying eyes, I ran my hands up the inside of his thighs, skimming them over the bulge in his pants. I could feel how hard he was, and though I didn't know what had him so excited already, I loved it. I started teasing him, running my fingers up one leg, quickly stroking his hard cock, and slowly going down the other leg before I started kissing him through his gray sweats. Gray sweats truly were a gift from all the gods. I looked up at him through my lashes and saw him staring intently at me. It was such a powerful feeling having the full attention of a man like Zane. It was its own form of intoxication. I could tell I was pushing the limits of his teasing, but I loved it. I continued to kiss his cock through his pants, wanting to see how much longer he would last before he snapped. One, two, three more kisses and he had my braids held tightly in his right fist. His tone was all gravel when he spoke. "Stop teasing, princess, and suck it like the good whore you are." The dirty words he spoke had me fighting a moan, always aware of the risk of our employees. Zane was impressive; his dark thick cock never failed to amaze me. He may not have been the longest, but damn he was thick and oh my god, did he know how to use it. As I pulled it from his sweats, I started licking slowly from base to tip. I knew I was driving him crazy and soon he would be full on face fucking me, and I could not wait. As I finally took mercy on him and brought his cock to my mouth, the door to the room opened. I didn't stop, but silently moaned, sending vibrations through him, loving this risky game we played. I had no way to see who was there so as I sucked, I listened. I heard Karma, our front desk girl, talking to Zane. She had no idea I was here under Zane's drawing table, with his cock deep in my throat. I wasn't really listening to what she said, but I heard her mention the name River and his cock jumped in response. Fuck. I couldn't wait to learn more about her; maybe he'd found someone for us to play with. I heard Karma leave and the door click shut behind her. I sucked harder, then let his cock fall from my lips. I ran my tongue down to his balls and sucked one into my mouth, knowing I was driving him crazy. I switched to the other ball before going back and sucking his cock aggressively. Massaging his balls and sucking hard was the end of him, his salty cum hitting the back of my throat as I greedily swallowed. I was always sad when his cum wasn't being used to breed me, but he'd just have to make it up to me later.

 I crawled out from under Zane's table and climbed onto his lap, knowing he'd want to return the orgasm, but also that he needed to finish this tattoo sketch. As I looked into his green eyes I saw the love and comfort that was always present. I felt at peace when I was in his arms. Finally breaking the silence, I said "Tell me about it?"

Chapter 3

Zane

Leave it to Raven to suck my soul from my cock and then immediately ask about the art that has me in a big knot. When Karma walked in-mid BJ- and mentioned River, I knew I was screwed. Raven could tell I had a reaction. I'd never hide it from her, I just wanted to wait to tell her after I had spent more time with River. But fate had different plans. I held Raven close to my chest as I responded. "She walked into the shop today looking for an artist. Damn, I was immediately into her. She had curves for days, a soft tummy that I wanted to lay my head on, and thick thighs with stretch marks. It felt like we were magnets, unable to stop the draw we had to one another. As much as I was drawn to her energy, I also couldn't stop picturing her going down on you as I pounded her from behind. And when she spoke, I was….. enthralled." Taking a deep breath, I rubbed circles on Raven's thigh, taking comfort in her familiar feel and warmth. "I don't think I'm ever prepared for how much we are able to help those in pain. River told me she witnessed her ex end his own life, though she didn't go into details. I want this tattoo to help her heal. I want it to symbolize everything she wants it to. She wants flowers blooming in ash and fire, with dog prints in the ash." I sat quietly for a minute, thinking,

CHAPTER 3

taking comfort in the familiarity of our bond. After sitting in silence for a bit, I finally spoke. "What would you think about the flowers blooming from the dogs' paw prints? I can tell her dogs mean alot to her. I bet the symbolism of her growing from their comfort would be meaningful to her." Raven met my eyes, hers flickering back and forth between mine before a smile started to pull at her lips. "You always amaze me with the thought and care you put into your art and tattoos. I love that idea. Would you like me to sit with you while you work, before my piercing client gets here?" I responded instantly, "You know I want you with me whenever possible." From there, Raven got off my lap and went to grab an extra chair. She sat quietly next to me reading something on her phone. I was sure it was smut, but her support and comfort meant the world to me.

I was looking at the design on my tablet, trying to decide where the paw prints with blooming flowers should be, when Karma came in again. She opened her mouth and then closed it slowly, eyes darting between Raven and I, and I could tell she was wondering where Raven had come from. She smiled warmly and turned to Raven, "I was coming to ask Zane if he knew when you would be in. We just had someone walk in for a piercing." Raven responded, "Tell them I'll be out in a few," and with that Karma went to get the customer's information and waivers done. Raven turned to me, "You've got this Zane. Your art is some of the best I've ever seen.... though Karma's starting to catch on." With that she shot me a wink and walked out the door.

With Raven out doing a piercing, I was once again left with my racing thoughts of River. The sadness and strength that came off her would forever be a part of my memory. I wanted this tattoo to show that, capture it, and make sure everyone knew a phoenix grows from the ashes... Phoenix? River hadn't mentioned one, but it felt so fitting to me. With that thought in mind, I decided I'd show her two drawings, both basically the same but one with a phoenix in with the flowers and paw prints. The gray and black with the pops of color would look absolutely phenomenal on her skin.

It had been three days since River had come in for her consultation and I could not wait to start her tattoo. Raven was standing with me at the desk, obviously enjoying how antsy I was. "Zane, I don't know that I've ever seen you this nervous to do a tattoo. Well, maybe that tattoo you did on me in my bedroom when we were 16 and our parents were right up the hall." I shot her a look for that comment; she knew how that ended for me. Our parents never hit us, but I lost all my privileges for a week, and somehow our dad got me doing community service. I actually enjoyed community service, but Georgia was too hot in the summer. I took my time before responding, "It's not very often someone speaks to me without words the way River did. I was drawn in and I know you will be too." I looked over at Raven whose long braids of black, purple, and blue came to just above her very grabbable ass. Raven looked like a walking wet dream in her ripped dark jeans, her black distressed t-shirt that read Vivid Ink, and black and white Vans. I was always taken back that such a stunning person, inside and out, welcomed my touch. I think Raven could feel my gaze on her because she turned her hazelnut eyes to me, looking straight through me and reading me like a damn open book as she always could. I decided an ass grab might just help my anxiety about River's tattoo. I leaned down and whispered in her ear as my hand went into the back

CHAPTER 3

pocket of her skinny jeans, "While I'm tattooing River's curvy body, I'm gonna be picturing her going down on the stunning queen now in front of me, while I rail her hard from behind. Seeing her take care of you like that is what I made myself come to in the shower last night. Your body shaking, biting your lips, arched back, and the moans," I groaned. I could see my words were impacting Raven, but now I also had a visible issue.... and Raven knew it. She turned to me and ran her hand up my cock. I knew this game we played was dangerous, but God did I love it. She looked at me, those seductive eyes grabbing my attention when she whispered back, "Be a good boy and maybe we'll be able to find out." It was then that the bell above the door rang, alerting us that we were no longer alone. She winked at me before turning to look at who had just entered our shop.

Chapter 4

River

Either my memory of Zane wasn't clear cause I was anxious when we first met, which is extremely possible, *or* he got hotter in a few days. Both were equally possible. I had decided that comfort was the most important thing today; I mean, I was letting a man shove a needle in my thigh over and over again. But also, said man was insanely hot, so I compromised. Black shorts that had lace on the trim and were extremely loose so they could be raised away from my thigh, a t-shirt where I cut the neck out that read **Smut Slut**. I dressed for comfort. Though I think the t-shirt added some spice. I did, however, do a full face of makeup to impress this man who was ten times out of my league. I mean, I'm a chubby white girl with *trauma* and he's...him. Though what I was not expecting was the stunning girl laughing and joking with him. Man, they were both so far out of my league it wasn't even funny. I fixed my expression, because I knew it probably showed jealousy, and went up to introduce myself to the bombshell.

"Hi. My name's River. I'm Zane's client today." She smiled warmly at me, immediately making me feel settled and accepted. It was a nice change of pace. She came around the counter to stand in front of me. "Hey! I'm Raven, Zane's partner. Can I

CHAPTER 4

give you a hug? Consent is super important to me." I could have cried and ruined my decent attempt at a winged liner. Being asked for consent before a hug was such a nice change of pace. So often they're just expected and taken. I nodded and thanked Raven. I'm pretty positive she could see how much that meant to me, if her eyes were that much of a window to her thoughts. Raven started walking toward Zane as she said, "Zane has been working extremely hard on your tattoo. I think you're going to love it."

The three of us started walking to Zane's room. I could not stop looking around at all the beautiful drawings. When I came in for the consultation, we never made it back to his room, so this was my first time seeing it. The walls were covered in beautiful drawings of different landscapes, some with the most stunning sunsets, beautiful portraits of different animals, and right above his drawing table was one of Raven holding a cat. That last drawing was staggering. I stepped closer to get a better look and I'm pretty sure my mouth dropped open. The drawing was mostly black and gray, but it had a few highlights of color; Raven's eyes, some of her braids were a beautiful forest green, and the cat's eyes, one blue and one green. I was speaking before I realized it. "This is absolutely amazing! You're truly talented, Zane. Raven, I know we just met, but I feel like this picture gives me a window to who you are as a person, and it's someone I would love to have in my life." I stopped short and bit my lip, "I...I...I can't believe I said that. Sorry if that was out of line." Raven smiled warmly, "Not at all. Based on your tattoo design, I bet we'd get along exceptionally well. I hate to meet and dip, but I have to go. Karma and I are headed to a Butch Walker concert. Have a phenomenal time, I cannot wait to see the finished tattoo!" Zane and I both said goodbye and Raven left.

I was still looking at the drawings when Zane started talking, so I turned to him. "River, I hope you're okay with me taking a little creative liberty. It just spoke to me..." He trailed off, seeming nervous? I quickly responded, making sure he knew I was totally okay with that and how I believed in trusting the artist. My reassurances seemed to help and he smiled at me. I walked over to him, excited to see the design. He went on, "I did two options for you; there is one big difference between them. I think I'll just show you both without an explanation and talk about my thoughts after." He pulled his tablet out and swiped through it until he was where he wanted to be. I looked over and gasped. The design was everything I could have asked for! An ash filled landscape, a beautiful yellow and orange sunset, three sizes of dog paw prints in the ash, and blooming from within the pawprints were a beautiful assortment of flowers all vibrant and healthy. Blooming from the devastation, just like I wanted. "Zane, I might cry. It is truly everything I could have asked for. It feels like my fresh start, me blooming from the devastation that my life became." Zane was behind me and I swear I could hear a smile in his voice when he responded, "I cannot tell you how much that means to me. Something about your story and tattoo just spoke to me. Can I show you the second option? It's the one that I took some creative liberty with." I nodded, unable to speak, my emotions running too high. He grabbed the tablet and switched to the next image and immediately I knew it was going on my body, no matter how much money I needed to come up with. "It's perfect," I whispered to him, blinking back the tears from my eyes.

Chapter 5

Zane

River had tears in her eyes and I was worried. She may have said my design was perfect, but the tears had me concerned. "Are you sure?... I see tears." River took a deep breath and looked at me, a smile on her face. "I mean it, Zane. It represents everything I need it to. I didn't even think to add a phoenix, despite them being a symbol of rising from the ashes. And hell, they're important in one of my favorite book series!" Zane chuckled. "Oh no! You love books and so does Raven. I can see y'all talking my ears off about the world of dark romance." River laughed and it was an amazing sound.

"Okay, let's get started. Do you need a drink? To use the bathroom?" River laughed at my eagerness and set a bag down in my extra chair. How I missed the bag before is beyond me; a canvas tote bag covered in different colors and sizes of titties and asses. "I feel like I should have noticed that bag before, but somehow I missed it. I was probably distracted by the two stunning women standing in the room with me." The blush that covered her face was what I wanted. She asked where the restroom was and walked out. While she was gone, I started getting my area set up. I knew this was gonna be a long, hard day for me, in multiple meanings of the word. My cock was already aching from the sight of her thighs in those short shorts. Hell, when she walked away I could see the curve of her voluptuous ass. I took the time to send Raven a quick text.

Zane: I am so screwed today

Raven: I know, I hope you enjoy it. I'll enjoy thinking about it.

Next, I received a picture of her favorite sex toy, a clit that often had her moaning in pleasure. I groaned audibly as the door opened, River walking in. "Is everything okay? I'm not sure I like the idea of being stabbed with a needle over and over again with someone who is audibly frustrated." I looked up at her, ready to ease her worries, but the small smile on her lips made it clear that she was just messing with me. "Everything is perfect and I'm excited to get started. Let's pick some colors for your tattoo." We picked out some vibrant reds and golds and some gorgeous purples, blues, and greens. I then instructed River to stand in front of me so we could put the stencil on. I got distracted staring at her skin and picturing what it would look like covered in my marks, whether the marks be from spankings or tattoos. I really had to shake myself out of the dirty thoughts and focus. When my mind was clear, I made sure to line up the stencil and place it on her leg. When it was on, she went and looked in the mirror. She didn't talk immediately, making my nerves start to take flight. "If you don't like something, please speak up. I want you to be completely happy with your tattoo." As she turned to look at me, there were tears in her eyes and a smile on her lips. She looked at me and said "I am so sorry to be such a mess today. This is really important to me. It truly symbolizes me growing and moving on. My life has been totally turned upside down so many times, and this feels like a pivotal point. I love everything about it. Thank you, Zane."

CHAPTER 5

The way she spoke those last three words did something to me. I couldn't even say what, but damn.

I started some music, ran to the restroom myself, splashed some cold water on my face, and headed back to the room. She was still walking around the space, looking at my art, so I stood there and watched her. I was sure she had no idea how beautiful she was. I cleared my throat before saying, "Are you ready to get started?" She smiled softly and nodded, turning to that tote bag of hers and pulling out three things: a book, something called *Saving Sorrow* by Kenzie Young, a water bottle, and a Coke Zero. She sat the two drinks on the floor near the tattoo table and waited for me to direct her. I had her sit at a slight angle with her left leg under the ring light. "Are you comfortable, ready to get started?" I wasn't sure why I was procrastinating. She nodded. I made sure the music was going to play 90's and 2000's alternative and got started.

I expected her to express a lot more pain; most people do when they get their tattoos. Hell, some of my tattoos had me on the verge of crying. River was just sitting there, reading, not phased by the tattoo needle. I had seen the few tattoos she had, so I knew she had some experience, but none of the ones I could see were even close to the size of this thigh piece. We were able to sit in comfortable silence after spending time earlier talking about our lives and getting to know a bit about each other. That's when I noticed she kept rubbing her eyes and temples. I needed to know what was bugging her and why. I put the gun down and she looked up asking, "Is everything okay?" Nodding, I said "I was gonna ask you the same thing, River. You keep rubbing your eyes and temples. Are you okay?" She only looked at me for a minute before letting out a small chuckle. "Yeah, I'm fine. I get chronic migraines and well, those are some of my tells. I'm totally used to them, so no need to worry. If it's gonna get so bad that I can't drive, I'll tell you and we'll pick a day to finish later. Though, if I'm honest, the feeling of getting a tattoo usually makes the migraine better." I could have sworn she winked with that last comment, but I couldn't be sure. "Alright, please let me know if you need anything, beautiful." My inner voice was screaming at me, 'What the fuck are you doing, dumbass?! You're gonna scare her.' Being this close to her was hard; my cock was throbbing and I needed some release. But I kept on working. The tattoo was coming along amazingly and River was sitting for it like a queen. I was about halfway through the tattoo when I heard it, her first moan. I put more ink in the tattoo needle and stole a glance. Either River did not realize she had moaned out loud, or she was ignoring it. I got back to tattooing and it happened again. Fuck. My. Life. I had to be professional, right? Right?! It was time for me to move closer to the top of her inner thigh. I could already smell her delicious scent and I knew it was only gonna get stronger. "Hey, River?" She looked up at me, confused, but consent was important. "I have to move higher up; I'll be all up in your personal space. I just want to be sure you're still comfortable with me." I was starting to love her shy smiles. "Yeah, Zane, you're good. Wherever you need to touch is fine." I couldn't tell if she was being flirtatious or just honest, but I was here for either one.

Chapter 6

River

Fuck, why had I decided to bring one of my favorite one handed reads?! Why was that smart?! Sorrow could tell me to do just about anything and I'd do it, never mind the fact that he's a fictional character in a book. I knew I had moaned out loud, twice. The vibrations of the tattoo gun, Sorrow's dirty words, and absolutely everything about Zane had me on the verge of doing something stupid. I wanted his hands on me, which was a big deal. I hadn't been comfortable with physical intimate touch in years. For so long, it felt unwelcome and dirty. I knew a lot of that was the guy doing the touching, which is why I got back into reading. The spice and love in the books kept me satisfied in my solitude, and didn't leave me with phantom hand touches for days after.

Just as I read about Sorrow grabbing Delaney's throat and whispering "shhh, you dont want anyone to know you're getting fucked in the bathroom like the whore you are," I shifted at the same time Zane shifted and his fingers grazed my center, causing me to deeply moan.

Chapter 7

Zane

I was panicking. I hadn't meant to graze her center, but I had and I certainly wasn't prepared for the fucking sexy moan she let out. I knew just from that quick graze that she was soaked. Her little black shorts were so loose I could easily see the black cotton thong she had on. God, I was in agony looking and not touching. What was this girl doing to me? Between Raven and River, I was gonna be hard for days. I looked up at her, only to see her looking back, a deep rose color on her cheeks. I opened my mouth to speak but she held a finger up. "Zane, can I tell you something? It's not professional, but damn I feel the need to." I nodded and waited for her to go. River took a deep breath and started speaking. "I'm not going to go into details but I want you to know, you're the first non fictional person in years that I've actually desired intimate touch from. I know that is probably TMI, but I think you need to know, based on me not being able to hide all my reactions brought on by both you and Sorrow," she finished with an embarrassed chuckle. I squinted in confusion, Sorrow? I was just getting ready to ask who Sorrow was when I remembered the name of her book *Saving Sorrow*. I smiled and said, "Smut. You and Raven will get along so well." She blushed harder and nodded.

CHAPTER 7

"Zane, I have a question for you." I nodded and got back to her tattoo. I had a feeling I knew what she was gonna ask and I didn't want eye contact making it too intense. River kept speaking, "Are you and Raven a thing? Y'all are so beautiful together and I could feel your chemistry earlier." I did a quick glance up, just to meet her eyes, before getting back to the tattoo and responding. "Yes, Raven and I are together." I quickly went on before she could get too caught up over that; I had the feeling she would immediately back off. "But, we're poly." I waited for her to respond, focusing on the quiet room filled with the humming of the tattoo gun and some alternative music playing. I wasn't sure what I expected her to say, but I was not expecting the words that came tumbling out of her mouth. She was talking so quickly, almost as if she didn't want to lose her will to continue. "Zane, this may be crazy, but I'm going to say it anyway. I haven't been kissed by someone that I wanted to kiss me in years. My last kisses were unwanted and forced on me, right before he shot himself. I hate that I can still feel his lips; would you take that away? You're the first person I have actually felt comfortable enough to want to kiss in I don't know how long." She took a deep breath in and met my eyes. I had pulled the gun away from her leg as soon as she had started talking, not wanting to get distracted and fuck up the tattoo. I looked at her for a long moment before making a decision.

"River, I would be honored. I need to text Raven first though, it's how our relationship works." She nodded and I quickly grabbed my phone, sending Raven a text.

Zane: Hey babe. This tattoo has suddenly had a slight change, she asked for me to be the first to touch her since the event. I don't know what all that means but wanted to give you a heads up.

I hit send and waited for a moment, it showed as read. Those three little dots that said she was typing appeared. In a very Raven response she said **"Go get her ready for me. We both know she'll enjoy me more later ."** I chuckled to myself, sending her a heart emoji and telling her I loved her.

I turned back to River, who was sitting up, nervously chewing on her plump lips. Her tongue darted out, wetting her lips. God, I wish it was my tongue . I could not believe I was going to get that honor. I was amazed, but I needed to make sure she felt safe with me. "River, I won't lie. I've been thinking of all the things I've wanted to do to you since you walked in. But I want to make sure you're good and that you know you're safe. Are you sure? I'm gonna lock the door; not to keep you in but others out. Karma and some of the other artists just walk in sometimes. But let's use the traffic light colors for how we're feeling and if you're ever uncomfortable, you say red. Do you know what I'm talking about?" River responded almost exactly how I expected her to. "I haven't used it, but I've read books with the traffic light colors used. If it's like my books, red is stop, yellow is okay but not great, and green is go/great. Is that what you mean?"

I took a deep breath before responding. "Okay, for today that will work. Just know consent is sexy and key. The moment you say red, we stop. I know it's just a kiss, but I want to be sure you're okay." The smile she shot me was one so full of feeling, it made my heart soar. "Okay, Zane. Come kiss me?" And with that, I wasn't gonna keep her waiting; my parents did raise a gentleman after all.

I moved forward and slowly looked into her eyes; one hand went into her hair, the other to her waist. I pulled her head to mine, foreheads resting together, our breaths mixing together as one. Her eyes fluttered shut and her breaths came harder.

CHAPTER 7

This stunning creature was asking me to kiss her, one of the most important kisses of her life. I took a deep breath and asked, "Color?" She moaned out the word "green", and with that I leaned forward. I took her lips in a soft caress, taking my time feeling how soft and plump they were. I pulled away to look at her eyes, looking for any regret or fear. There was none. She leaned forward and took me in a hard kiss. Tongues dancing together, hard breaths, quiet moans, as her hands started to roam and I let them. I kept my hands where they were, though maybe the hand in her hair gripped it hard, harder than the kiss called for. I needed more. I pulled away from the kiss again. "I wanna touch you, is that okay?" She moaned and nodded. "Not good enough, beautiful; words of consent, please." The moan that left her was hotter than most porn stars fake moans. "Yes please, please touch me."

If I hadn't already been hard and leaking precum, those words and moans would have brought me to full attention. However, I had been there since she walked in the goddamn door in those shorts. "Okay beautiful, first, I'm gonna put gloves back on and wrap your tattoo up. Don't need you getting an infection or anything. How about you tell me about whatever you were reading; I bet it was hot based on those moans." I was captivated by her voice as she talked about her book. It sounded hot. Apparently a plus sized girl was getting absolutely railed in the bathroom of a club. I'd definitely have to tell Raven about this book. Once I had her tattoo covered, I took my gloves off, locked the door, and walked to her. "Color?" She bit her lip before saying "green", and with that I was on her. "That's my good girl. Tell me how wet you are." Through kisses she said, "I'm fucking soaked. I need your mouth on my clit. I wanna come." I liked this bold side of her. I could see she seemed shocked by her own words and I was not going to let her mind get in her own way. I didn't need to be told twice. I took off her shirt and tossed it across the room, pulling her bralette down under her tits. God, they were a perfect, overflowing handful with hard, rosy nipples. I groaned as I tasted them, taking them in my mouth one at a time. As I finished tasting both nipples, I started kissing down her stomach, soft under my hands. I could feel the stretch marks and could sense her sucking in. "Don't do that princess. You're incredible the way you are. I don't ever want you to hide your stomach or marks from me." With that, I kissed her, before continuing to kiss down her stomach. When I made it down to her shorts, I looked back up. I didn't even need to ask. She moaned the color "green" again, and I pulled her shorts off leaving her in nothing but her little cotton black thong and bralette pulled under those tits. I leaned down and went straight for her clit through her panties, and she lifted her hips trying to get me closer.

I took that as my cue, pulling her thong off and impulsively, sticking it in my pocket. I leaned over the tattoo bed, ignoring the pain from my knees on the hardwood floor. I started teasing her, kissing up her right leg slowly, starting at her ankle and making it all the way to her thigh, where I blew a hot breath on her most sensitive area before starting on her left ankle. The light moans leaving her mouth were so sexy, because she was actually comfortable and enjoying my mouth on her. I sucked hard on her clit while sticking one finger inside her. She was tight, so very tight. I slowly started working my finger in a come hither motion, getting her ready for another finger. When she was ready, I entered a second finger and started moving them both, massaging her inner walls. As my hand worked, I started sucking her clit before stopping and moving my tongue over

CHAPTER 7

it in a fast rhythm, before sucking hard again. I could feel her pussy walls fluttering on my fingers and fuck, I wanted to feel that on my cock. I worked her clit and walls until she came, hard. Legs shaking, low moans, and breaths coming fast. I kept working my hands and mouth until she rode the wave all the way out and she gasped about how she was too sensitive. I sat back on my ankles, a triumphant smirk on my face, before I stood to lean over her and kiss her hard. The kiss was still just as frantic and hot. Suddenly, her hands were rubbing my length through my pants and she said, "Will you fuck me? Please Zane? It's been years since I've felt this sexy and desired." Who was I to turn down such a beautiful, strong woman?

Chapter 8

River

I was struggling to catch my breath. One of the sexiest men I have ever seen, just gave me the best orgasm. Hell, I don't even think my trusty clit stimulator, bedside boyfriend, gets my clit that good and sensitive. But I was ready to be fucked. I was tired of knowing the asshole that shot himself in front of me was the last man in me. And Zane? Zane just felt right. He kissed me again and I could taste myself on his lips; fuck that was hot. He leaned forward, pressing our foreheads together again. It was comforting and I craved touches like this. Touches that were gentle, caring, and not full of rage and control. I kissed him again, closing my eyes before he could see me cry. I didn't want *him* to ruin my time with Zane; *he* didn't get to take away this happy feeling.

Zane pulled back and smiled at me before some fucking hot and naughty words left his mouth. "I want to see that big ass bent over my desk. I wanna watch my thick cock pounding in your tight cunt." Fuuuuck, I was done for. He kissed me again, before helping me off the tattoo table and towards his drawing desk. He kissed me hard once more and asked me for my color. I said "green" and he quickly turned me around and pushed me over his desk. With one spank to my ass, he entered me from

CHAPTER 8

behind. The feeling of his thick cock inside of me was almost more than I could handle. It had been so long since someone was in me and I was loving it. He slowly started moving in and out, getting me used to the feeling and size of him before he started to pound faster. I knew this was gonna be a quick fuck, we did have a tattoo to finish after all.

He pounded me hard from behind and started to move his hand around 'til he could find my clit. I didn't want his fingers there, so I pulled his hand away from my clit and put it on my nipple. His other hand was still gripping my ass hard. I was enjoying the sensations from his hands on my body, while he continued to pound me like the world was ending; maybe it was. After a few more minutes, I could feel him groan as he came. We stayed like that for a bit and he started to kiss down my back. I waited for him to ask why I had moved his hand, but he didn't and I was so grateful. Maybe he could tell I wasn't ready to talk about it or maybe it wasn't as weird as I thought, but he didn't ask and that was all that mattered. Suddenly, the tears came. I was unable to hold them back and Zane's arms were around me. This poor man, who was only supposed to give me a tattoo, was now holding me like nothing else mattered.

Chapter 9

Zane

River was crying and fuck, was I worried. Everything had seemed fine, but I also knew this was a big deal. The more I held her, the more I realized the tears should have been expected. She was sitting on my desk now, not bent over it, and my arms were wrapped around her as she cried into my chest. My t-shirt was getting soaked, but I had no intention of moving her. She needed this and even though we were nothing before today, I could feel that changing. Hell, maybe I needed this too, to feel someone cry in my arms like this. Raven and I cried together when needed, but I can't remember the last time one of us had a need to cry like this. I held her tightly, letting her get all her feelings out in a safe space. You never knew what you were gonna get while tattooing; people's emotions run high. They get tattoos for different emotional reasons and reactions can be intense. That was one of the reasons we designed the shop with individual rooms with doors that shut. Too many studios lacked privacy by having one big room and some movable dividers.

River's tears were slowing down, but her breaths still came hard and fast. I continued to hold her, rubbing circles on her back, giving her any and all comfort I could. I didn't dare tell her everything would be okay. I didn't know her well enough for that and empty promises could really hurt. I was planning on keeping River in my life, even if it was only as a friend. I liked her and I could already tell she and Raven would be trouble together, but in the best way. Though I was a little worried for our wallets with book and audio book purchases if they become friends; it sounded like they both were real book lovers. "River? What can I do? I want to be sure you're okay. We can finish the tattoo another day if you need to go home." I waited as River took a few big breaths before shaking her head on my chest. "No, I'm green for the tattoo." The color reference brought a smile to my lips. "Just let me run to the bathroom and clean my face off. Guess I no longer need to look good anyway." I frowned at that statement as she unlocked my door and went to the bathroom. What did she mean by that? I planned on finding out but wanted to be gentle about it.

When River walked back in, her eyes were red and puffy and her cheeks pink. I could tell she had scrubbed all the makeup off her face and she looked defeated. Life had obviously not been kind to River, and I only knew a part of it. While she was in the bathroom, I cleaned myself up and got the tattoo equipment clean and ready to be used again. I was slowly realizing this had not been my most professional day; fucking my girlfriend in here was one thing, but a client?! I shot Raven a quick text.

Zane: Hey, just checking in. About to get back tattooing. I'm realizing this wasn't professional and I wish I could say I regret it, but I don't. I think she needed it, especially with her break down after. I'll tell you more at home. Does that make me a shit man? Would you be okay with me creating a group chat with you, me, and River? I think she could really use it. Love you.

I decided against waiting for a response; she'd respond when she could and right now River needed me. When I looked up, she was biting those delicious lips and shifting back and forth from one foot to another. "Zane...." she started before stopping. It was obvious she had something to say even if she didn't know what, and I had a suspicion she wanted to apologize. I walked over to her and took her hand, guiding her back to the tattoo chair, where she had a perfect sight of the desk we'd fucked on.

"Please don't apologize little dove. I wanted you, from the moment I saw you, but I wasn't about to push you. Hell, Raven wants you too and I'd love nothing more than to have both of you." River just stared at me, obviously having no idea what to say, so I continued. "But for right now, let's finish this tattoo and not stress about everything else." River let out a deep sigh and I could tell that was what she wanted to hear. She already had so much going on in her life, she didn't need to feel guilty for asking for my help to move on. Sure, I was definitely curious as to why she moved my fingers off her clit, but if everything went my way, I'd be learning all these little things about her as we dated.

All of a sudden I realized, "Shit, River I forgot a condom. I'm clean, as is Raven, but I was just so in the moment I didn't even think. Raven and I don't use them." River looked at me, sitting quiet and worried on the tattoo chair, before she finally responded. "Zane, I'm clean; there's no need to worry about that. I have PCOS and am not on birth control, but it should be hard for me to conceive. I mean with my weight and PCOS, my body fights against shit like that." I hated her comment about her weight, but wasn't sure how to bring up the topic. "Well little Dove, all that matters is we're both clean and healthy. Now let's get this beautiful thigh piece finished." For the next few hours, we sat in a comfortable quiet with nothing but the

CHAPTER 9

alternative music playing in the background. She picked her phone back up and started reading again, without the moans this time. Either I had satisfied her enough or the book wasn't nearly as spicy as it had been earlier, but logically I knew that wasn't the case. Somehow, I just knew her past was lingering close to the surface and the spice in her book wasn't getting through it.

We were approaching the end of the tattoo and I knew I needed to make a move. "River, I want to ask you something." I waited for her eyes to leave her phone and meet mine; she tilted her head sideways and I knew she was listening. I went back to tattooing as I spoke, thinking it would make it less awkward if I wasn't looking directly into those pain filled blue eyes. "I'd really like to take you out. Hell, I'd love to take you and Raven out together. I know she'd love to talk about books with you. I know I want to learn more about you, as does Raven. What do you think?" I waited, adding the finishing touches to her tattoo, giving her a chance to answer without any pressure. When she finally responded, it was in a quiet voice, and my heart pounded quicker in my chest. "I'd love that Zane. But y'all have to know, I come with multiple loads of baggage and trauma. I won't dump it on you, but I won't be an easy anything. Friend. Lover. Partner. I'm working hard to overcome everything, but I do not want to put it on others and be even more of a burden than I already am." Halfway through her response, I looked at her. Just watching, in awe of this beautiful woman, who had been through so much and who handled it in a stronger way than most would have. "River, I am in awe of your strength. Instead of you facing this world and future alone, let me be there. I'll be one of your shoulders to cry on, one of the people encouraging you. I'll be there so you don't have to fight the fight of life alone." I left it at that before telling her the tattoo was finished. I cleaned the area, using the dreaded paper towel wipe at the end of a tattoo, and told her to stand up and go take a look.

Chapter 10

River

"Alright, River. I just finished cleaning your tattoo. Can you stand and walk over to my mirror to take a look?" I just nodded. I knew if I spoke he'd be able to hear the tears and break in my voice. I hated that I always felt like a problem, so I hid my tears so they would not burden anyone else. I slowly walked over to the full length mirror on his wall, in awe over the designs he had covering the outline of the mirror. His talent was clear to see. I hadn't looked at the design a lot as it went on my skin. I wanted to be surprised with what colors had gone where. When I was finally standing in front of the full length mirror, I gasped and covered my mouth, holding back a sob. It was beautiful, absolutely everything I could have asked for.

On my left thigh was a beautiful blue and purple sunset over an ash covered ground. In the ashes were three different sized sets of dog paw prints and all the paw prints had different flowers blooming from them. Some of the flowers were just starting to bloom and others were in full bloom. It was a perfect representation of how I felt about myself. But the part Zane had added to the design, made the representation so much more. Flying through the sunset was a phoenix, its red and gold feathers standing out. The entire design represented beauty blooming and growing from the ashes that hurt so much. I would likely always have PTSD; the memories would always be there. But I was blooming, growing, flying into a brand new beginning. And I could not help but hope I had found someone, or two someones, who would help me flourish.

"Zane...." I trailed off, unable to put into words how much I loved it. How much this tattoo meant to me. "Zane," I started again, "I'm struggling to find words that tell you how much this means to be. You captured everything I wanted from this tattoo, and then some. I absolutely love it! And I would love to go out with you and Raven sometime, if you still want to." The smile that came across Zane's face had fucking butterflies fluttering all over my stomach. Holy shit, butterflies. *Butterflies.* When was the last time I had those bastards?! Certainly not recently. Years? I don't even remember having them when I met Cam. It suddenly felt like a rock landed on the butterflies and made my stomach ill. Fucking Cam. No, he didn't get to take this from me. "Thank you, Zane. Truly. I can't wait to show it off." We walked up front, I paid, and we hugged goodbye, with promises to all hang out soon. But all the while, my demons were gaining some serious ground. Zane told me to reach out, but as I walked out to my Jeep, I knew I wouldn't. Two people that stunning, don't go for a fat widow with trauma out her ass. I knew my insecurities were getting to me, but I also knew that I was a lot and didn't want to bring them down, so I'd distance myself. Besides, he was in a happy relationship and just because two people fucked, didn't mean they actually had a connection, even if the connection had felt real.

I was really excited to show off my tattoo, so I decided I'd

CHAPTER 10

head home and show my parents. A lot of people would be embarrassed about living at home at 30, but not me. Hell, even without my situation, living at home wasn't a bad idea. But with my trauma and Cam leaving me with debt and work tools to sell, it was my best option. Besides, I worked at a daycare. Who the fuck could afford to live alone on a day care employee's salary?! I had only been able to continue to do the work I loved because Cam was our breadwinner. Now I can only keep doing it thanks to my parents. I drove from the tattoo studio in Atlanta, Georgia to my childhood home in Lilburn. The drive could take anywhere from 40 to 60 minutes depending on traffic, but it was well worth this beautiful tattoo.

I parked my old beat up Wrangler outside my childhood home, a large, light green house that obviously was not a typical cookie cutter style home. I called my dad as I pulled into the driveway. Having to navigate dogs was a pain in the ass, but it was well worth it. Our dogs couldn't be together because of aggression, so once he assured me that it was safe for me to let my mutts out of the house, I let my three pit mix rescues into the backyard. Roddy was a big black pit bull who only wanted food and hugs. pit bull was my large tan pit mix who just wants all the pets, and Bates, a large brindle pit mix, just wants to be with his mommy all the time. Bates was also affectionately called my terror, Roddy a garbage disposal, and Matty-Ice a hippo. And yes, I did name my dogs after Falcons' football players.

Once my dogs were in the fenced backyard, I went in search of my parents. They were both very supportive of me, in every way, shape, and form, and understood my desire to get a tattoo. I hadn't told them what I was getting, so it was gonna be a surprise, especially the size. I found my parents in their room, surrounded by dogs, watching some Netflix show with ghosts.

They paused the show as I called out and walked in, a blanket I had grabbed off the couch wrapped around me. They shot me strange looks, making it clear that they were confused. I mean, as a very hot natured person, wearing a blanket around was weird. But I wanted to hide my thigh till the last minute. It was a surprise after all. I paused for a moment to enjoy the comfort that the sight of my parents brought me. I got my curves from my mom, though she was more fit than me, and her hair was currently dyed a burgundy color. My dad was skinnier, but I looked more like him; our face shapes and noses were the same, though his hair was a natural salt and pepper. Laney and Blake were good parents; they voted blue, were supportive, and very understanding. I really was extremely lucky in that way.

I walked in and turned their light on without warning, earning me two loud "fuck yous" from both parents, and dropped the blanket. They blinked in confusion for a few seconds before mom saw it and gasped, loudly, causing my dad to jump a little. "Oh, River. It's beautiful! I think it's perfect and symbolizes absolutely everything you wanted it to. I am so happy for you." I sorta wished my dad wasn't in the room. I wanted to tell mom about the progress I had made in being touched. It was a big deal, but I knew my dad didn't want to hear about his daughter being eaten out and railed mid tattoo appointment. Luckily, my dad could tell I needed some mother-daughter time and said, "I love it, it looks great. Looks like it hurts like hell, but looks great. I'm gonna go sit with the barking Falcons so y'all can talk."

Chapter 11

River

R I sat next to my mom on her bed and decided I needed something soft to cuddle. It was then I noticed their cat, Carl, on the pillows behind me. So, I grabbed Carl and forced his orange ass to cuddle me. My mom waited patiently while I worked up the courage to tell her about this huge hurtle I jumped today, though I was a little worried she was gonna judge me or maybe accuse Zane of using me. I let out a deep sigh and started, "Mom.... this might be an awkward conversation, but I need and want to talk about it." She nodded her head and I went on. "One of the things I've been struggling with most since his suicide, is touch. Not like hugs, but touches from people I'm interested in, romantically." I stopped there, taking a minute to compose myself, as the next words were gonna be harder to tell her than the actual railing that took place. "One of the reasons I have really been struggling with it is...my last kisses, hugs, and anything intimate were not necessarily consensual. I didn't explicitly say no to Cam, but it was clear I was uncomfortable and pulled away. Hell, he forced me to do some things I definitely didn't want. One of the moments I cannot get over is when he shared a video I didn't know he took, where he tied me up and blindfolded me against my will.

He shared it without my permission." I took a break there, blinking back tears and trying to compose myself. I knew that if I started to break down, so would my mom. I did not need her to break down more than she would at the news of my last intimate encounters being, well not really consensual. She grabbed my hand and squeezed, giving me the courage to keep going. "Because of those experiences, I have had a really hard time with letting a date touch or kiss me. A hug, no problem, but a kiss?! Intimate touch?! I have not been comfortable with it. But something about Zane," my mom cut me off and asked who Zane was, so I answered her question. "Zane did my tattoo. He owns Vivid Ink with his partner, Raven. They're poly and one of the cutest couples I have ever seen." She nodded and motioned for me to continue. "Anyways, something about Zane is different. I immediately felt drawn to him. Hell, I was drawn to Raven too but I didn't get to interact with her a lot. But, something about Zane made me feel relaxed and safe. I also was reading *Saving Sorrow* and that book is **hot**." She chuckled at that and rolled her eyes. She knew I loved spicy books and occasionally she'd steal one of mine to read. Maybe I should lend her *Saving Sorrow*. I realized I had gotten distracted and tried to rein in my wandering brain. "Anyways the book is fucking hot and I love spicy books with a plus size FMC." She gave me a confused look, so I explained "FMC is short for female main character. I love spicy books with characters that look like me. It makes it more realistic and hot. Anyways, I was reading the first scene between the two main characters and I was really enjoying it. Something about the situation made me brave and I asked Zane if he'd kiss me." She looked absolutely stunned at that news. "I know, right?! Anyways, he didn't just kiss me as soon as I asked. He asked if I was sure and made sure I had a

CHAPTER 11

safe word in case I started to panic. He made sure I gave him explicit consent, which is hot, and even texted his partner to get her consent." I took a few moments to see if she'd respond and when she didnt I went on. "It was the safest I have felt in an intimate situation in a very long time. I am so happy I was able to overcome this fear." My mom still did not respond immediately, so I prompted her. "Mom?"

It still took her a minute to respond, but I didn't want to rush her. Hell, I had just essentially told her someone she considered a son, had pushed my consent away and used me. When she finally responded, it was slow, like she was thinking about each word before she spoke. "Okay, River, so you're telling me you were in a relationship with someone who did not always ask permission before doing something intimate or personally invading. They would just invade your personal space and take what they want?." She stopped and waited; all I could do was nod. I knew this was gonna break her heart. She had so badly not wanted this experience for my sibling or I. It was something she was all too aware of and the damage it could do. She shook her head and appeared to be gaining her composure. "And those actions have held you back since becoming single?" I responded to her question as honestly as I could. "Trust is hard for me, especially with a lover. I trusted Cam. Was supposed to be able to trust him with everything, but he broke that trust. He broke that comfort. So, it's taken me a while to feel I'm in a safe place with trust and comfort."

We were quiet for a little while. It was obvious my mom needed time to process. Carl was purring loudly on my chest, and his soft sounds and vibrations were relaxing me. I really needed to pee, but I did not want to move Carl, and mom and I were having this deep conversation. I didn't want to break it.

"So," she began, "Zane made you feel comfortable? And safe?" I knew I needed to respond with words, a nod didn't seem like enough. "Mom, I cannot explain how comfortable and safe I felt. It was so strange to be that close to someone I was attracted to and not be wondering where their hand was gonna end up. So, I asked Zane to kiss me. It felt right."

While I was not religious and didn't really believe in fate, my mom did. So, I knew she would take that as something deeper than I meant it. But a small part of me wanted to think me going to Vivid Ink was fate, like I was supposed to be there. But this was not Solaria. I wasn't at Zodiac Academy, the stars did not influence us like that. I didn't feel the need to tell my mom anything else, so we just sat there for a while. Eventually I laid my head on her lap, while Carl laid his head on mine, and tried not to think about Zane's cum inside me while we watched whatever crime show she wanted to.

Chapter 12

Raven

I had waited all day for details. The thought of Zane being with River had my leggings wet all afternoon. Besides, he owed me from the head the other day. While I waited, I thought about what I wanted to do when he got home. All I really knew was that I wanted him to tell me how much of a good girl I am while I sat on his face. I decided to call Zane and see if he had any idea on how late he would be. That way I would know how much time I would have to get prepared for him. I hit the contact named "teddy bear" on my phone, finding the pet name perfect and funny. Almost no one would describe a man like him-covered in tattoos and intimidating-as a teddy bear, but it was accurate. Zane was the most cuddly penis having person I had ever met.

"Hey butterfly," Zane answered as he picked up the phone. "How's my girl doing?" I bit my lip. I just loved Zane and the way he made me feel so much. It may have taken our parents a little bit to be okay with our relationship, and the poly aspect as well, but once my dad saw how well Zane treated me, he was on board. Zane's mom wasn't as convinced, but eventually my dad talked her over. Now they saw us the way we saw us and it was everything. "Butterfly?" I realized I had gotten distracted."

Hey baby, sorry. I got distracted thinking about how much I love you." I heard him chuckle over the phone and it brought a smile to my face. "I've been thinking a lot about you today too. How was the rest of your day?" I didn't want to go into details about my day; nothing had really happened and I needed to know about his day. Whenever one of us gets some, we have a great time talking about it. It's one of my favorite conversations with Zane. We can talk about who was and wasn't able to get me off. Who was a good or bad ride for Zane, and so much more. So I blew a breath before responding.

"Stop trying to distract me, Zane. My day was nothing to write home about. I want to know how your day was and what time you think you'll be home?" He full on laughed this time, telling me "I know exactly what you want to hear. My good girl better be naked and laying on the bed when I get home. I want to see you playing with that pretty pussy when I walk through those doors in 10 minutes. Get ready." And with that he hung up and I got down to business. I quickly took off my socks, leggings, and t-shirt and put them in the hamper. I went to the bathroom, needing to pee mid face sit, sucks dirty ass. I also quickly freshened up. I have this bad habit of assuming Zane won't want to touch me if I haven't just cleaned myself. Logically I know that's some bull shit, but my intrusive thoughts occasionally win.

Fuck, I am so ready. We had been together just yesterday, but it never feels like enough with Zane. He's my addiction and I don't ever plan on going to rehab. I made sure my braids were fanned out on our blue satin pillowcases, as I lay naked on our gray blanket. I started to play with myself, slowly working myself up. My fingers circled my clit, slowly rubbing it. As I brought my other hand up to my tit, flicking my pierced nipple,

CHAPTER 12

I moved my other hand lower, gathering my wetness. I brought my wet fingers up and slowly moved them over my clit, it felt so good. I knew just how wet I was and the thought of Zane coming home to this, made me even wetter. I let out a moan and squeezed my tit. Fuck, I wanted Zane's hands on me.

Chapter 13

Zane

Once I got off the phone with Raven, I was ready to be home. I knew neither one of us would want to cook, so I placed an order with our favorite pizza place. We love that we can select a delivery time, so I gave us an hour and a half before dinner would arrive. From there I was out the door. Raven and I only lived a few miles from the shop in a small, 3 bedroom, 2 bath house. We had bought it the same time we bought the shop. As I walked up the street I smiled as I thought of our little home. It was simple, cute, but it fit us and I loved it. I stopped thinking about our home and started thinking about the girl in it. I knew my good girl; she would be on our bed doing exactly what I asked her to do.

When I finally made it home and slowly opened the front door. I didn't want Raven to know I was home yet. I wanted to sneak into the room and watch her touch herself. I couldn't wait to see those slim fingers running through her pussy lips, smell her sweet scent, and hear those moans. Those moans were mine tonight, and no one else's. Sometimes hearing her moan for someone else is hot as hell, but not tonight. Tonight, all her moans and noises were mine. They were for my ears and cock only. I ran a hand along my hard length through my pants, as

CHAPTER 13

I slowly shut the front door. I saw our cats, Truth and Dare, sitting there, looking at me. I groaned. I was gonna have to feed them or they would never leave us be.

I walked quietly into the kitchen and decided to treat the cats. If I grabbed their hard food there was a chance Raven would be able to hear it, and I did not want her to know I was home yet. So I went into our pantry and shut the door behind me. I grabbed two cans of wet food and opened them in the pantry, hoping she wouldn't have been able to hear any of that. God, this shit smells, but Truth and Dare love it. I slowly and quietly exited the pantry, put each cats' food in their individual bowls, and washed my hands without making a lot of ruckus to distract Raven from her task. If Raven is being the good girl I told her to be, she would be too distracted to pay attention anyways. I started down the hall, being sure not to move too quickly and cause the floor to creak. After a few steps I heard it. One of my favorite sounds in the entire world; Raven's moans. Those moans were the first I ever heard and if I had my way, I would hear them for the rest of our lives. I made it to the door, which was mostly open, and leaned in the doorway, watching. I saw her fingers moving slowly over her clit, glistening with her desire. Fuck, she was beautiful. Her dark skin always stood out so well against our blue and gray bedding, and I'm reminded how fucking lucky I am. This goddess before me chose to be mine 12 years ago and every day since. How did I get so fucking lucky?

I walked slowly into the room, ready to taste what's mine. I planned on making her come on my tongue and my cock. Kneeling before the bed, I kiss the inside of her left knee, startling her from her task. "Hey butterfly." I greet, nipping the spot I just kissed, causing her to yelp in surprise. She lightly smacked my cheek, the only place she could reach, while giggling. "Hey you," she gasped back through breathy moans as I licked her entire slit. She's soaked and fuck she tastes good. My butterfly liked a little pain with her pleasure, so I planned on providing some sweet pain with her pleasure.

I sucked her clit, hard, then nipped at it before sucking again. The varying sensations had Raven moaning, as I pulled away and blew on her clit, slowly pushing two fingers inside her. I stretched her tight pussy, getting it ready for my thick cock. As I found her g-spot, I got back to work on her clit. I wanted her over sensitized, begging me to stop from how good it felt. I was alternating between sucking and biting her clit, working her most sensitive area hard, determined to get her over the edge fast. Raven started to buck her hips, her hand on the back of my head holding my mouth to her clit, a sure sign she was about to come. I kept at it, breathing be damned, and was rewarded with the holy grail. Her moans were soft, but filled with pleasure, and her legs were shaking. I licked her through the climax, keeping her pleasure peaked. When her legs stopped shaking, I kissed her clit, blowing on it for fun, before I crawled over her. I kissed random spots of skin, causing chill bumps to appear. When I finally made it to her mouth, I gave her a dirty kiss, the taste of her moving between our tongues.

I pulled away from her mouth and touched our foreheads together. "I missed you, butterfly. She grins at me, a goofy grin that shows how happy she is and it makes my heart smile. I am so content in her arms; convinced that I am luckier than I deserve. "I cannot tell you enough how much of a goddess you are, Raven. You are my everything. My future. I love you." I kiss her again, before rolling us over so she's straddling me, rocking her hips over my length. Raven smiles back, before telling me she loves me too. Continuing to rock her hips over my length, we both groan. She's so wet and I'm hard as steel.

Raven leans down to kiss me again, and between kisses she asks me for details about what happened with River. I know the dirtier I make my words, the more she'll enjoy it. "I wanted to feel River's legs shaking and her pussy clenching around my cock. I wanted to tease her until she begged me to fuck her." Raven moaned as I pulled her down harder on my cock, her clit rubbing on my length. "I kissed my way up her legs, teasing her clit through her little black lacy thong. It was so soaked." Then I remembered her thong is still in my pocket. Making an impulsive decision, I turned back to Raven and said, "How badly do you want a taste of our beautiful River?"

She looks at me like I have lost my mind, "How am I gonna do that? Did you decide to surprise me with her?" She looks behind me, like she expects to see River walk through the door. I chuckle. She knows I wouldn't do that without her permission. "If you want a taste, close your eyes and open your mouth." After a few seconds, Raven does as asked. With her eyes closed, I quickly grab River's thong out of my pocket and lay it on the bed. "You're being such a good girl," I gasp in Raven's ear, causing goosebumps to crawl all over her skin. "Such a good little slut for me, waiting to taste what I got to taste earlier." I quickly take off all my clothes and crawl back up her body. I kiss randomly all over her body, loving the shivers that result. She doesn't know where I'll kiss next, if it will be a kiss or bite or pinch, and the anticipation is building her excitement. For a moment, I just stare down at her. Her breaths are coming heavy from her parted lips, her eyes closed, her lips slightly swollen and wet, and a flush has entered her dark cheeks. She's stunning like this, waiting for my cock, excitedly waiting for me to tease her. Without warning, I lean down and drop a quick kiss on her open lips, before grabbing River's thong, balling it up, and stuffing it in Raven's mouth. Her eyes fly open and I can tell she was not expecting me to have taken River's thong and certainly was not expecting it to end up in her mouth. As I look into her eyes, I slam my cock in her dripping pussy. The sight of her laying on the bed, River's thong in her mouth and my cock in her pussy, has me ready to come.

Chapter 14

Raven

My eyes shot open and I let out a surprised, yet muffled, gasp. I wasn't expecting her thong to be shoved in my mouth, though I am definitely not complaining. In all honesty, I was expecting him to thrust his cock down my throat. I expected to be able to taste them together, but something about feeling his cock in my pussy while tasting her juices on the thong, is so incredibly hot. The thought of Zane teasing River through these panties he has shoved in my mouth, is so hot it has me ready to shatter all over again. Zane has always known how to press the right buttons for me and since we've been exploring kink together, he's gotten that much more skilled. That much hotter. That much better with the words that will get my pussy soaked and waiting.

Zane slowly starts thrusting in and out, getting my pussy ready for him to take me hard. As he thrusts, he continues to tell me about how he made River come with his mouth, and as he works to make me come, I'm reminded that I am tasting the arousal of the woman he pleasured earlier, leading me to moan again. It is so hot. I am so lucky. Zane moves onto his knees, pulling my legs over his shoulders and the new angle has me feeling so much more of him. He continues to pound into me, hitting all the right spots, as he tells me about him taking River from behind over his drawing table. He starts rubbing my clit and all the different sensations have me shaking, my second orgasm drawing closer and closer, before I shatter and moan Zane's name through my lacy gag. He's not far behind me and as I hear him groan, he drops my legs and leans down over me. To my surprise, he doesn't take the gag out but starts kissing down my body, occasionally sucking, leaving my body littered with hickeys. He makes it to my center, holds my eye contact, and licks my entire slit. He tastes us together and the thought has my pussy clenching on nothing. The dirty smirk he sends my way tells me he knows what he's doing to me. He shoots me a dirty wink, before going down on me until I shatter again. Afterwards, he comes to lay next to me in the bed. My eyes are closed but I can feel him staring at me from above. Sweaty skin, flushed cheeks, and a lace thong in my mouth, I feel beautiful and used. It is such an intoxicating feeling. Zane takes the thong out of my mouth and gives me a quick kiss, before getting up from our bed.

I am so tempted to pass out in the wet mixture of us that is on the sheets, but Zane is not about to let me sleep in a wet spot. He wants to take care of me too much. He walked into our bathroom and started running a bath, which I am sure he already has at the temperature I like, with my rose scented bath salts and bubble bath. I rolled over and hid my giddy smile in my pillow. I dont need the cocky fucker's head to get any bigger. Those thoughts had me giggling to myself.

I can hear Zane walking back into the room and feel him sit on the edge of the bed. When I don't immediately move, he starts rubbing a gentle hand up and down my back. "As much as I love the thought of my cum staying in that pretty, breedable pussy, I

CHAPTER 14

need you to move, goddess." His pet name for me always makes me feel amazing. He continues talking, seemingly oblivious to the back flips taking place in my stomach. "Why don't you go to use the toilet, we do not need you getting a UTI, and then hop in that bath and let it relax your body. I'll take the wet sheets off the bed, start them in the washer, and put new sheets on, before hopping in the shower. I do need to check and remind myself when I scheduled our dinner to arrive." I just nod, before taking his hand and letting him lead me into the bathroom. Zane leaves to give me privacy and take care of the rest of our needs for the night.

Turns out our dinner had been delivered sometime during our fuck fest, and we just never heard it. Zane put it in the oven on low heat, just to keep it warm, while we both got clean and ready. The bath felt amazing on my body. With a book playing in the background and my braids protected from the bath water in a purple shower cap, I could have stayed in that tub for hours, but my stomach growled and it became clear I was gonna have to get out sooner than I wanted. I let the water out of the bath and joined Zane in the shower. I always shower after a bath. Why would I not wash off the dirty bath water filled with my filth of the day?

I loved showering with Zane. He was just such a comforting presence, and he was happy to let my book play as we gently washed each other. Zane grabbed my purple exfoliating net and put my rose scented body wash on it, before scrubbing down my entire body. I did the same to him, but using his musky body wash on his blue exfoliating net. He took the shower head off the wall before rinsing us both off; it's the perfect end to the day. Zane shut off the water, giving me a quick kiss before grabbing two bath sheets. And yes, I mean bath sheets. Bath towels are only big enough to dry hair, not an entire body, and I refuse to believe any grown adult actually likes the size of a "normal towel". We each dry off, my audiobook still playing. Once Zane was dry, he put on a pair of boxer briefs and walked out of the bathroom, calling over his shoulder to sit on the bed once I'm dry. I decided comfort over being cute is the way to go tonight, so I put on some oversized sleep shorts and an oversized t-shirt before sitting on the bed.

I turned my audiobook off before turning on the TV that's hanging above the distressed teal dresser on the wall across from our bed. The cooling sheets feel amazing against my freshly washed skin. I turn on YouTube and navigate to the Mythical Kitchen channel. Zane and I love to watch Josh and the entire crew work their magic in the kitchen. Queuing up a fancy fast food episode, I pause it and wait for Zane to return. He soon comes into the room, with two plates and two cans of Coke Zero. I am once again struck by how lucky I am. Not only do I have this beautiful person to call mine, but he also takes the time to take care of me. We ate our dinner while watching the Mythical Kitchen and once we were done, Zane took our dishes to the kitchen and put them in the dishwasher. I washed my face, put on my nightly creams, and brushed my teeth before climbing into bed. Zane followed soon after and crawled into bed with me.

We weren't big nighttime snugglers, since we both sweat a lot in our sleep, so we gave each other a soft kiss before rolling over and getting comfortable. Zane was used to falling asleep to one of my comfort books. Tonight was *Bound Spirit* by H.A. Wills, Zane knowing it's one of my favorites. He proved how well he pays attention by telling me how much he hoped Callie and the guys will bring me comfortably into sleep. We both drifted off

CHAPTER 14

to the drama of Callie learning how to be a witch correctly.

Chapter 15

River

That night, I ran the day over in my mind. I can't get over the fact that I let someone touch me. The last person inside of me is no longer *him*; I feel like a new person. Like the fresh start I wanted with my tattoo is right around the corner. It is so close I can feel the breeze of it brushing up against my skin. I decided I need to get out of my own head and try to continue reading *Saving Sorrow,* but all that does is remind me that I was reading it earlier before Zane touched me.

I spent a few more seconds looking at the ceiling, before I said "fuck it" and pulled out my trusty clit stimulator. Between thinking about Zane and Sorrow, I was soaked. I scrolled back to the same scene I was reading earlier, the one about Sorrow taking control in the bar bathroom, and slowly brought my toy to my clit. The sucking sensation, the remembered touches from Zane, and the words on these pages,have me reaching my climax quickly. It felt a little more empty than the climax with Zane did, but I know it's going to be how I finish for the foreseeable future. Zane may have hinted that both he and Raven were interested in talking to me, but I kinda doubt it. I know my personal insecurities and doubts were causing me to spiral and have self doubting thoughts.

CHAPTER 15

    I have a lot of trauma and a lot of baggage. I'm too much for someone to handle. I know I have issues, so many issues...I was kind of planning on being alone for the rest of my life. I didn't want my shit to bring down the lives of others; no one in my life asked for that. It's not worth it. I fell asleep with those words floating around in my head, as some audiobook played in the background. I didn't even know what book I put on, my thoughts were just too loud.

It had been a couple of weeks since I got my tattoo and I had received several texts from Zane. I hadn't responded and I felt really shitty about it. I was currently in the waiting room for Dr. Alex and I wanted to talk to her about what was going on. Logically, I knew she was going to call me out for self sabotaging, but that broken part of me was sure she was going to validate my fears. The part of me that's constantly yelling about how I'm a burden and not worth anyone's time, care, or love. The waiting room for Dr. Alex was quaint, a pale pink color with several comfortable black chairs everywhere. I was feeling so anxious that I couldn't even concentrate on reading a book. My legs were bouncing and I was twisting my hair like there was no tomorrow. I am far from okay. Suddenly, the nerves got to me and I told the receptionist I had to go to the bathroom. I barely made it before my stomach emptied itself. God, I was not expecting therapy to get to me this much today. Oh well. After my stomach decided it was empty enough, I stood up, washed my hands and face, rinsed my mouth out in the sink and headed outside. When I opened the door, I saw Dr. Alex standing there, eyebrow raised, clearly asking me what was wrong. I shrugged and just looked at her. I know she could see the pain behind my eyes, I'm not even trying to hide it today. Today, the demons are winning.

My session with Dr. Alex was a mess. I was a mess. My life is a mess. The words "terminal illness" are scrolling across my vision, like you see on the big screens at sporting events. It's funny, I may have been miserable in my relationship. I may have felt more like a mom than a partner, but I at least had someone. No matter how poorly they treated me, I had someone. Sometimes, the pain of the abuse kept me going. It was consistent. I knew he'd be there. I knew he'd yell and then buy me ice cream to say sorry. The comfort of his vile words was no longer there, only making me more aware of how broken I was. The more I realized I took comfort in the familiar abuse, the more ashamed I felt. I should have been stronger. I should have left years ago. The "should haves" and "could haves" controlled a good bit of my thoughts.

Dr. Alex and I had been sitting quietly for a few minutes. I think she was giving me time to process what I had just told her. I explained how glad I was for my experience with Zane and that I was so glad the last body part to touch me wasn't His, but I had also explained why I wouldn't reply to Zane's texts. How I am too much, too broken, and too much of a burden. No one deserves the pain that is me. No one deserves the mess that is my life. Dr. Alex finally sighed before speaking. "River, I am proud of you. Allowing someone else to touch you was a huge step, and it seems like you actually liked him. Am I correct?" She waited for me to nod my head in confirmation before continuing. "I know that you feel like you're not worthy of anyone. I know you have described his words to be like shovels digging away at the person that you are. But do you really think all of this is to protect others from you, or are you protecting yourself from the pain of rejection? To protect

CHAPTER 15

yourself from the chance of being hurt like that again?" I knew she didn't expect an answer. I knew I needed to think about her statement and have a response for our next session.

As I walked out to my Jeep, a vehicle I have grown to hate, I found myself in tears. The silent tears that will become racking sobs to violently shake my body soon enough. I knew I'd break the moment I was officially alone. I knew the moment I closed my Jeep door that I'd be hyperventilating, sobbing, and ripping my hair. It's all too much; I'm too much. I decided it was time to take a first step in improving, so I shot Zane a text.

River: I'm sorry for not responding sooner. I have been fighting some personal demons. If y'all are still interested, I would love to get together.

I didn't expect a quick response, so I turned the phone on do not disturb. I mean, I'm a millennial. I can't turn the damn thing off, I'd lose my mind! I sit and just cry. I cried until my throat and eyes hurt. I cried until I realized I need the comfort and safety of my mutts, and they're not with me in my therapist's parking lot. They were at home, waiting for me to come to them. With those thoughts, I started my Jeep, took a few big gulping breaths, and started driving.

I had Spotify playing on random and I wasn't really listening to the music, but more had it on as background noise. It was so weird to me that I could feel like I was shattering with the hurricane of emotions, but everything else in the world appeared bright and shiny from first glance. I knew everything in the world was far from fine: capitalism, billionaires, racism, sexism, genocides, colonization, and so much more. So many people, constantly shattering, but outside it was sunny and beautiful. Maybe I should blame global warming.

I stopped at a red light when I realized two things: I needed a fountain soda and I hadn't checked my phone. I had a weakness for a Coke Zero from the fountain; they're the best and my drug of choice. I decided I needed to pull into a gas station, get a fountain drink and text my parents. They always liked to hear how I was doing after therapy. They hated knowing the trauma their little girl went through. I was waiting in the left turn lane for my green turn arrow. It was a fairly busy road, so my chances to turn left weren't all that frequent. When my light turned green, I started to turn left, when suddenly there was a big crunch. I heard things breaking and saw multi-colored stars flashing before my eyes, when suddenly everything went black.

Chapter 16

River

The next few hours, I floated in and out of consciousness. My reality went from being black and silent, to the loud and abrasive sound of sirens and worried voices. The flashing lights hurt my eyes so I kept them shut tight and tried hard to block out the sirens and loud voices. My head was throbbing, I was nauseous, and it was all too much. Too much sensory overload. Next thing I knew, everything went black and there was no more noise ringing in my ears.

Next time I came to, everything was still black, but I could hear a lot of worried voices. I couldn't quite make out what they were saying, but I could sense something was wrong. I wanted to know what was going on, why everything was still black, why there was ringing in my ears, and why everyone I heard was so worried. I felt like I could faintly hear sirens still and I wanted to know why. It was while I was thinking about all these questions, that I started to fade again. I came in and out of the black a couple more times. At least once, I could tell I was rocking and had no idea why. The last time I came to, I could tell I was on a stretcher. I didn't know what had happened, but I could tell I was being wheeled quickly down a hall. The bright lights of the hospital and the smells were my first clue as to where I was. As I was wheeled down the bright halls, I was slowly realizing just how absolutely awful I felt. My entire body was achy and sore. I felt like there were tiny cuts covering my body and fuck, was I dizzy. The walls and rooms appeared to be rushing by. I knew it was me rushing by, but that wasn't how it looked, and I was starting to wish I was still blacked out. At least then I wouldn't be so dizzy and on the verge of emptying my stomach. I tried to keep my eyes closed, but I was finally able to talk to the nurses, which was a relief. I only managed to tell them how sick and dizzy I felt, before I laid my head back down and concentrated on keeping my eyes shut as much as possible. The nurse next to me was a plus-sized lady. I made a mental note to ask her name, though I wasn't sure I would remember. She had on those hospital green scrubs, but she was working them, and she handed me a blue circle bag. It took me a second to realize I was concentrating on her ass and not the barf bag. I finally peeled my eyes away from the distraction and grabbed the barf bag. My brain finally seemed to realize I was lifting my head and neck at a weird as fuck angle, which hurt, and I laid it back down on the pillow. Why I was originally laying on my side, holding the guard rails, and lifting my head is beyond me, but my brain was doing weird things. I kinda realized that maybe I had a head injury and that's why my brain wasn't braining.

I finally felt the bed slow down and eventually stop. I decided it was safe to open my eyes. There were three people in my room, all varying levels of tan, and all working quickly. The plus-sized lady from earlier introduced herself as Dr. Green and told me I was in a car accident and had been rushed by ambulance to a local hospital. The other two people introduced themselves as nurses. Nurse Jacob had a nice smile on his face like he could tell just how thrown I was by all of this, while Nurse Dakota was all business informing me that they use they/them pronouns and they'd be here to help with whatever I needed. I liked Nurse Dakota. The fact that they so proudly told me their pronouns brought a small smile to my face. I think that their take no shit attitude would be good for me. I tend not to speak up for myself, but something told me they'll see right through that and force me to be honest.

Dr. Green was a short, curvy woman with dark brown hair and eyes that were a deep shade of brown, which shone with kindness. Her shade of brown skin was beautiful and I kinda wanted to ask about her skin care routine because *gah damn*. Nurse Jacob was a skinny man who was rocking some shaggy blonde hair and light brown eyes, filled with laughter. Nurse Dakota was as pale as I was, covered with freckles, and light green eyes that drew me in. Not in the "I'm attracted to you" way, but in the "did we just become best friends" way. Something about them just soothed my soul. I could tell just from the vibes that I was gonna like my care team.

I jolted as I realized I'd been zoned out, not actually listening to what they were asking me, which was probably important based on how they were all looking at me expectantly. "Ummmm," I said lamely, before deciding to be honest and continuing. "I wasn't listening. What did y'all ask me?" Dr. Green chuckled in a soft manner before asking her questions again. She asked if I could remember anything that happened, how I was feeling, if I had any major areas of concern, and of course the dreaded "are you pregnant?" question ovary people had to get asked at any doctor's appointment. I took a second to think about my answers before I responded. "I have flashes of a car accident, but I don't have one set memory of it. More like random flashes of sound and light." I also told her I was very sore, especially on my left side, and that my brain was fuzzy. I quickly answered the last question, "I'm not pregnant. There's no way. I haven't had sex in years." It took me a moment to remember that wasn't true. "Wait, I don't think I can be pregnant, but I forgot I had sex about a month ago." I shrug before continuing that it just wasn't the most relevant thing in my mind. Before they could continue down that line of questioning, I decided to quickly ask my own question. "Did someone grab my phone from my car? I was on my way home and I am sure my parents are worried." I half expected some judgment; I felt judged a lot of the time when I tell someone I live at home, but there is none. I let out a sigh of relief. I really hated that because of society, I felt obligated to explain my living situation to random people. Like, why do people have to care about an adult woman living at home? As if the price of living isn't insanely high. Is that not reason enough? No? Why does society need my trauma? Why do I need to give them a detailed reason as to why I live at home? It's not their business. I shook my head and realized I'd gone off on society in my thoughts. It happened a lot because everything was so fucked up.

When I finally cleared my thoughts away from how much the United States-let's be honest though, when has the US ever been united-sucks, I realized Nurse Dakota was waiting for me to realize that they were handing me my phone. I mumbled a rushed sorry as I grabbed my phone from them. I was tempted to wince prematurely, kinda convinced they were about to hand me a shattered phone screen, but somehow my Samsung is fine and I'm glad, because I do not have the time or brain power to worry about my phone. I thanked Nurse Dakota before

CHAPTER 16

searching for my dad's contact. He almost always answers his phone, while my mom forgets she has one. I listened to my phone ring twice before I heard my dad's comforting voice. It's like just hearing his voice helps me calm down. "Hey Dad," I say, trying to come up with the words I need to tell them what happened. I continued with an "ummmm" that seemed to tell him something was wrong.

"What is it? Are you okay? Shouldn't you be here by now? I'm just now realizing you never called me to see if you were able to let your dogs out." I let out a small laugh before I answered his questions. "I think I'm okay?" I know there is a question in my tone, but I continued talking before he could interrupt to ask me questions. "I was in a wreck. I don't really know what happened, but I am at the hospital." He quickly asked me what hospital they needed to come to before I heard him yell for my mom to get ready to leave. "Dad," I say, but he doesn't seem to be listening to me, so I repeat myself a little more loudly. "*Dad!*" That time he realized I was talking and started listening to me again, making a questioning sound to tell me he's back. Before he can ask a bunch of questions I don't want to answer over the phone, I quickly ask him if he will let my dogs out and feed them before they head this way. He agreed and told me he'd see me soon. I really wish I could have asked him to bring one of my dogs; they're such a comfort for me. I could really use their comforting presence, since my life has been turned upside down AGAIN in less than two years.

Chapter 17

Raven

I know Zane was disappointed that he hadn't heard from River. He seemed to really like her. I was honestly surprised by how much he seemed to like her. Zane had only ever really been able to bring a third into our relationship in a sexual manner, but this felt different. I'd been with other emotionally connected partners, but he hadn't. I had been his constant for most of our lives and I kinda wanted to hate River for doing this to him. But I was aware that River had a lot of inner demons and likely faced them day in and day out.

I knew our parents, and honestly some of our friends, did not understand why we like poly (or ethical non-monogamy) in our relationship. With the way Zane had been acting the last few weeks we, mostly me, had been answering a lot of questions as to why we liked non-monogamous relationships. I was really over it. I was texting my friend Dakota. Dakota had always been more of a "I'll do it myself" kinda person, and the idea of them using someone else for emotional comfort, seemed ridiculous. But I loved Dakota. They have been by my side through the entire rocky mess of Zane and I getting together, and I owed them all my feelings. Usually they understood the basic idea of not being with just one sexual partner, but the part

CHAPTER 17

they didn't understand was putting their heart in the hands of multiple people. Like, how was one partner supposed to give you everything you needed sexually?! That was logical to them, but add in emotions to the mix and they get confused.

I took a deep breath, reading over Dakota's text for the third time. They asked if I wanted to go get a drink with them later and talk about my feelings surrounding Zane and River. I kept reading it to see if I could detect an undertone of being judged. But honestly, I knew better and Dakota didn't judge on shit like this. I knew it was the echoes of our parents and friends that had me questioning the undertone of Dakota's text. I finally shook the thoughts out and asked them to come over after work. I didn't feel like going out, but wine and pizza at home sounded perfect. I just needed to make sure Zane knew it was a Raven and Dakota friend night. He knows what I mean when I say that and doesn't get upset when I need friend time. I was always so grateful for his understanding because I had heard horror stories from women and their boyfriends.

Over the next several hours I cleaned and maybe got a head start on the wine while I waited for Dakota to get here after work. Dakota was my best friend and they kept some of their clothes here along with showers and random beauty products, because they often came over after work. We wanted them to have a safe place after not having one for years. By the time Dakota got here, I was feeling the wine, probably because I was irresponsible and didn't eat before drinking - oh well. Dakota rushed to the shower to wash off the day from the emergency room. While they were in the shower, I went on to a delivery service app and had the local pizza place bring over three pizzas. I ordered Zane's favorite 5 cheese, Dakota's favorite veggie, and my favorite BBQ chicken, then proceeded to swipe through

TikTok and wait. Zane had told me he'd stay in our bedroom tonight unless I asked him to join. I was so thankful that he understood my need for comfort from someone else and it didn't impact our relationship. In the middle of watching a bunch of funny orange cat behavior videos, I heard "Hey bitch. Save me any wine?" I laughed, handed Dakota a glass, and put my phone away.

Dakota looked exhausted and told me about their day in the ER; apparently it was a day full of car accidents. Dakota told me most people were released after a few hours, but they thought the last person would still be there when their shift starts in the morning. The patient hadn't been hurt enough to rush them to the over-occupied ICU, but she was going to need a good bit more testing that would likely take some time. Mostly because she needed a CT scan and it was so backed up today. I laughed as Dakota rolled their eyes, because their ongoing beef with the CT scan department always amused me. My laughter was quickly cut off when they shot me a look that told me they knew I kept asking about work to distract them from asking about Zane.

I sat up straight and got ready to tell Dakota about River. I wanted to get through it quickly before they asked questions, so I asked them to wait with questions till I was done. They nodded that they understood. I took a deep breath and started. "I have wanted Zane to be able to connect to another, emotionally, for a while. I think it will help him grow and learn more about himself. Hell, we have been together for so long I think he is missing out. I have had other emotional partners and it has been so much better for me. I mean, how is one person supposed to handle all the other person's shit?! It is so much easier to spread the shit between others, and yes I know friends do that, but you cannot deny you usually tell lovers and friends different things.

CHAPTER 17

Different people bring different things to relationships and it helps them grow and be stronger." Dakota nodded, having heard me give this rant too many times and they asked about the person Zane seemed to be hung up on.

I told Dakota about River and the tattoo Zane did for her. I saw them frown, almost like they knew who River was or they were trying to place the name to a face. But that can't be possible. I have never heard Dakota mention anyone like River before. I told Dakota about how River witnessed her partner's suicide and how the trauma of her relationship made physically intimate touch really difficult. I went on telling Dakota how Zane said there were immediate sparks between them and how River asked Zane to be the first to touch her and how big a deal that was. It was at this point that Dakota stopped me, focusing on the wrong part of my story. "Raven, are you telling me that when I got my tattoo from Zane a few days ago, I was sitting where their bodily fluids were?!" I chuckled as I shook my head. "Why are you focusing on the most irrelevant part of my story?! You know Zane cleaned the fuck outta that room. He takes the safety of those he tattoos very seriously." Dakota let out a deep breath at the same time my phone told me the pizza was here. I brought Zane his pizza upstairs, where he was watching YouTube, and gave him a quick kiss before heading back down to Dakota. We talked and drank while eating the amazing pizzas. Dakota didn't really ask more about River, but decided to tell me about this person they had recently met at a play party. Something about this encounter told me that this may be more than a fuck buddy, but only time would tell. We were having a great friends night, when it suddenly sounded like there was a stampede of hippos running down the stairs. We looked up to see Zane and the cats running down the stairs like their lives depended on it.

Chapter 18

Zane

I saw both Raven and Dakota looking up at me like I had lost my mind. They knew our cats were heathens, but I guess this was more than normal. As I walked past them, I held up a finger to signal them to give me a minute. I knew I needed to take a second and get my shit together before talking to Raven and Dakota. Raven would get it, but Dakota kept their emotions behind a shield and I didn't want to push mine on them. I hadn't yet told Raven that River had texted me earlier. I wasn't keeping it from her, but since I hadn't heard from River again, I thought it wasn't important. However, the text I just got explained why she had texted me and then went radio silent. She was in the hospital. She had texted me to work things out and then was hit by a car. I didn't have all the details, but I knew I was going to head to the hospital. The text apologized for disappearing while she was in the hospital. She should be worried about herself, not me.

Once I caught my breath from running down the stairs like a mad man and had taken a moment to gather myself, I walked back into the living room. Both Raven and Dakota had their eyebrows raised in the exact same way, asking me what the fuck was wrong with me. "So," I started lamely, trying to figure out what to say next. They both gave me impatient looks, so I decided to just talk to Raven. Dakota would understand that I wasn't trying to be rude, but Raven is my comfort and I needed her. "I heard from River earlier today," I finally say. Before she can ask why this is the first Raven has heard of it, I continue, "she texted me to apologize for not responding to any of my texts, that she had been working through some shit." Raven nodded, showing me she understood, and by the way Dakota was looking at me, I can tell Raven told them about River. "I texted her back telling her I understood and I really want to see her again. Then radio silence. I just assumed she freaked out again, but…" I trailed off, not knowing how to continue. My feelings surrounding River were complicated; I really like her, but she hurt me by disappearing. However, I knew that was about her and not me. But how was I supposed to know it wouldn't happen again? Raven spoke up. "But what? Are you gonna tell us the rest or do we need to guess what's going on in that confusing head of yours?" I laughed, because Raven always knew what to say. "She's apparently in the hospital. She was in a car wreck today." It was at this point that we were both startled by Dakota saying, "Shit, I was hoping it wasn't the same girl who came into the ER today." I blinked at them, stunned that Dakota had already been wondering if she could be the same girl. Dakota couldn't tell us any personal information because of the law, but we decided to all go to the hospital. I was a little worried the hospital staff would ask Dakota why they didn't mention knowing River earlier. When I turned to Dakota to ask them if it was a good idea for them to come, they stopped and just waved their hand in dismissal, obviously not concerned. I was consistently surprised by their ability to read my mind and not stress.

CHAPTER 18

    We cleaned up the pizza, wine, and wine glasses in the living room, not wanting the cats to get into any of it. I shut the door between the kitchen and living room, keeping the cats out of the kitchen while giving them access to all the toys and furniture. We all got into my car, since the other two were too tipsy to drive, and headed towards the hospital. As we drove, I noticed Target coming up ahead of us and made an impulse decision to turn in and make River a care bag. Within minutes I was kinda regretting bringing them, especially to Raven's happy place, as they were both a handful when tipsy. But they were happy, helping me make a bag for this girl that I didn't know well, and I instantly felt guilty about my regretful thoughts. They both cared for me so much, and I was really grateful. While browsing, they kept asking me random questions about her. I told them she was a plus sized, smut loving, Coke Zero girl. With that, they were off. I picked out a lilac colored canvas bag with a rainbow on it to put everything in. I also grabbed a stuffed cat. I knew River had dogs, but I have cats and I kinda wanted her to have something that represents me in the bag. I found the other two in the book aisle and picked up one by an author I had heard of before, but never read. They both quickly told me that the displays with "SJM" and "CoHo" were a no-go, due to being problematic. I blinked at them, obviously confused before Raven took pity on me and explained that those are the authors' names abbreviated and showed me their books. We ended up picking a beautiful looking book by Shain Rose called *Between Love and Loathing,* before we paid and headed to the hospital.

    Once we got to the hospital, I was so grateful Dakota was already over when I got the news. Their name at the hospital made it possible to just walk right in and straight to River's room. One of Dakota's co-workers joked that they just couldn't stay away from work. They talked to their coworker for just a moment, while Raven and I waited awkwardly to the side. After they confirmed that River was still in the same room, we were on our way.

I wasn't sure what I expected to see when we walked into River's hospital room, but I was glad to see she wasn't alone. An older white couple was sitting with her talking. River was sitting up in bed, but looked to be covered in small cuts, bruises, a black eye, and her right arm was in a cast. Dakota hadn't warned me about how she'd look and I was taken aback. This beautiful woman who I'd had the pleasure of touching, looked so hurt. Almost like a small amount of the inner scars she hid, are showing on the outside of her body. Her door was open, but I still knocked to let her know we were there. When she looked up at the sound, I could see the surprise on her face. River quickly introduced us, telling her parents I did her tattoo and we were developing a great friendship. She went on to explain how I had listened to her and she hadn't felt judged, which she feels frequently. The older couple decided to make their exit, hugging River and kissing her cheeks before telling her they'd care for her mutts tonight. They shot River a knowing look on their way out of the room. The three of us stand to the side and wait while trying not to be intrusive.

Once they left, we all walked in. Raven and Dakota sat in the chairs the older couple had just occupied, while I walked over to River's side. I leaned down to kiss her on the cheek, while I tried to come up with the right words to say. This beautiful, strong, woman who had dug her way into my heart. What did I say to express how glad I was to have heard from her and that she was okay? I finally settled on just being honest; honesty is always the best policy. "River," I started before the words died on my tongue. I tried again. "River, when I got your first text today I was elated. I am really looking forward to getting to know you. I was worried when I heard you were in the hospital, but luckily Dakota was already over when you texted me. It is such a lucky coincidence they were able to figure out what happened. We all came as soon as we could. How are you feeling?" The small smile she gave me made my heart beat quicker in my chest. When she finally responded her voice was raspy, like she strained it screaming. "I'm a little sore. Just waiting on blood work to come back. I finally got my CT scan and I have a concussion along with a broken wrist, bruises, and cuts. Oh, and I need a new car. The asshole that hit me totaled my Jeep." River took a breath for a moment, like she needed to gather her thoughts. "I'm really okay, ready to break the fuck out of this place though. Fe will be here soon, and he's gonna get me home safely." I was glad to hear she had someone coming to get her. We smiled at each other, before I realized Raven and Dakota were waiting for us to include them in the conversation.

I finally remembered my mom raised me with manners and said, "You remember my partner, Raven, from the shop?" She nodded her head, before telling Raven she was glad to see her again. "And Dakota tells us y'all met earlier today?" River chuckled and nodded, saying "Dakota was a great nurse. They cared a lot. Hopefully I wasn't too much of a pain in the ass earlier." Dakota assured River that they did, in fact, care and that she was no problem. Then Dakota joked about River obviously enjoying the view earlier. The color that flooded River's cheeks told me the statement was true and my interest peaked. I quirked an eyebrow and River's cheeks darkened, before she said something about Dr. Green. "Ahhhh," I said.

"I know exactly what you mean. We've met Dr. Green a few times when we visited Dakota before. I would have enjoyed the view too." That earned me a playful spank from Raven and I turned over my shoulder to wink at her. Just as I turned back to River, there was a knock at the door and a Doctor I hadn't met before walked in. He greeted us, but it was short and rude, before he turned back to River. I could see the way she shrunk back from this man, her posture telling us how uncomfortable and scared she was. Why was she scared of this doctor? Unless I was reading her wrong, but I didn't think I was.

The doctor was an older white man, with brown, balding hair, a pot belly, and he reeked of cigarettes. I knew my face was showing I didn't like this man and Raven's was showing the same dislike, but Dakota looked murderous. Before we could ask for an introduction, he turned to River and started in on her about her weight; how she'd be better right now if she lost about a hundred pounds. My blood was boiling and I was ready to let this man have it. How dare he?! River is in here because of a car accident, not her weight. Dakota quickly spoke up. "Dr. White, why are you loudly talking about River's medical information in front of other people? She did not know we were coming, so there is no way she has given you permission to speak so openly about something related or unrelated to her car accident." There was a moment where no one spoke and this man, this Dr. White, sneered openly at Dakota.

I was ready to defend everyone here, but I also knew Dakota and what they could handle, so I leaned back against the wall to watch the show. Dakota had a hard life and learned quickly to take no shit from anyone. When Dr. White opened his mouth, I knew it was not going to go well for him, at all. "Listen, Nurse Dakota," he used so much venom on their name, I'm surprised

CHAPTER 18

he didn't have snake fangs. "I just want to know who knocked River up, because it can't be my son. She's the reason he's fucking dead." There was a stunned silence, during which no one knew what to say. Did this man really just say that? There were suddenly wracking sobs coming from River and I rushed over to her. I held her as close to my chest as possible, letting her tears soak my shirt. This man was the dad of her late partner, and he......my thoughts drifted as I focused on the two words I'd heard earlier. "Knocked up?" I ask. I see the color drain from Dr. White's face. I turn to River, knowing the answer to my question before I even ask it. "Did any other medical staff tell you that you were pregnant before now?" She shook her head and Dakota turned to Dr.White.

Chapter 19

Raven

The words "knocked up" were flashing in my vision. The room was quiet, apart from the beeping of different machines and the sobs muffled on Zane's chest. So many thoughts were racing through my mind right now. Who knocked her up? Did she lie to Zane about not being able to have other people touch her? Is.... is it Zane's?!

I knew the answer as soon as I thought of it; it's Zane's. I could tell River wasn't the kind of person to lie about something so intimate and I could tell this news was ripping through her, like a tornado in a trailer park. I had to work to not lose myself. I wanted a baby with Zane, but the timing hasn't been right. Right now, the shop was our baby. These intense feelings of jealousy were raging through my body. I was aware it's ridiculous as I'm absolutely certain River wasn't planning on a child so soon after her partner's suicide. I worked to get my emotions in order, telling myself I'd take time to feel them later, as right now we needed to handle this Doctor. I knew Dakota was going to lose their mind when it came to Dr.White's actions. This was a severe breach of privacy.

CHAPTER 19

I watched Dakota get up and slowly walk over to the doctor. They looked like a big cat stalking their prey, getting ready to pounce. I enjoyed seeing Dr. White cower under the stare of Dakota, this man who obviously thought the world would do whatever he needed it to. Dakota looked like Dr. White was about to be their new favorite meal. They spoke in a low voice, one that River wouldn't be able to hear, and told Dr. White "You and I are gonna walk out of this room. You're not going to say anything else to River, and we are going to go tell the admin what you just did and you will be completely honest. The patient in this room is already traumatized enough from her car accident, to the trauma your son put her through when she witnessed his suicide. If you truly loved and cared for your son, you would love and care for the woman he loved." With that, Dakota took Dr. White out of the room. I looked over to see River still crying into Zane's shoulder and I kinda felt like I was intruding on something private. I suddenly got up and headed over to the door, my eyes meeting Zane's and he nodded in understanding. We'd talk about this when we got home.

Chapter 20

River

I still couldn't believe he said that. I knew he didn't like me, so that part wasn't a shock. I was never good enough for his blue collar son. I'd always felt his disdain for the woman with curves, rainbow colored hair, and tattoos that his son brought home. But I couldn't believe he just announced medical information I hadn't even known, to a room full of people! I was in so much shock it took me a minute to realize Zane and I were alone. At the thought of his name, it hit me. He just found out he's gonna be a dad. My inner panic was strong, so strong that I knew I was on the verge of a panic attack and needed to keep it together. Zane needed me to keep it together. I could be the strong one. I don't break. I witnessed my partner end his own life. His dad being an ass to me while I was in a hospital bed was not going to break me. But I already knew I'd lost this battle. I was breaking down and maybe, just maybe, I needed to break. And maybe, it would be ok if I was safe in the arms of someone to hold me while I broke.

Chapter 21

Zane

Listening to River cry was killing me. I could tell she was trying to hold the tears back, but I didn't want her to. I wanted her to feel safe and secure in my arms. I didn't know what about this woman drew me to her, but something just felt so right about holding her. I knew eventually we'd have to talk about the pregnancy, because I doubt she had let anyone touch her after me. Just the thought of another man touching her had me seeing red. I took a few deep, calming breaths. It suddenly hit me....I was gonna be a dad? I could hear the question in my own head. I didn't know how I should feel about it, but my initial emotion was happiness. Apart from the man who would never be known as "father-in-law of the year", that is. I didn't care what her relationship with her late partner was; if you'd been together a while, you consider them your in-laws.

I was still holding River as close to my chest as possible. I could feel the hurt radiating off her. I knew she was trying to push her emotions down, like she didn't want to put them on anyone else, but that was not about to fly with me. I wanted those feelings. All of them. I wanted her to feel them and not push them so far down, that no one would be able to dig them up. Even if our relationship went nowhere, I'd be there to pull her out of the grave she had dug herself into. Though, I knew I was going to be pushing for a real relationship. I wanted this girl in my life.

As I held River, I started rubbing soothing circles on her back with my right hand while my left made its way into her hair. As I started stroking her hair, I heard a soft moan leave her. Did my girl like her hair played with? I kept it up, comforting her in every way possible. It took awhile before there was a knock at the door. I moved so I was sitting behind River, her back to my front, so we could both see the door. I continued to offer comforting touches, as I didn't want those gut wrenching sobs to come back. She had finally calmed down and wasn't bawling anymore. Silent tears were making their way down her cheeks, and I kissed one away. She told whoever was knocking, to come in, and I prayed to whoever is up there that Dr. White didn't walk through that door. Luckily, another doctor walked through and I kinda already approved. She looked like a take no shit, cool ass grandma. She had a hot pink streak in her short salt and pepper hair, and the scowl on her face said she was out for blood. I could only hope she was out for Dr. White's blood. River greeted the newcomer, her voice strong, with no evidence of the breakdown she just had.

"Hello. I'm Dr. Williams. Are you Miss Collins?" After River confirmed that she was and asked for Dr. Williams to call her River, the doctor continued. "River, Dakota informed me of your interaction with Dr. White." I feel River suck in a deep breath at the mention of that dickwad, but the doctor continued without missing a beat. "I want to assure you that it will not

CHAPTER 21

happen again. He has been escorted off the property and will no longer have access to this hospital. Do you have any questions or concerns that I can address?" River nodded, it was clear to me that she was steeling herself to say whatever was coming next. "I..." River started, before trailing off. "I wasn't aware I was pregnant before he told me. All I knew was I was in a car accident." You could see Dr. Williams soften and she nodded her head before answering River's unasked question. "I'll order an ultrasound, just to check, and we'll do some additional blood work. Better safe than sorry. Give us a bit and someone will be here to get y'all shortly. I'm assuming this is the father?" I didn't have a chance to respond, before River turned to me and in an extremely light voice said, "Zane, I guess I'm pregnant, and if I am, I know you're the father." I chuckled and kissed her cheek. Even through this bullshit, she was smiling and trying to make me laugh.

When Dr. Williams finally left, River turned to me. "Zane, I truly had no idea about the baby. I am so sorry you found out like this. I don't know what any of this means, but know I don't expect anything at this point. We really don't know each other and I don't want to burden anyone's life." With that statement, she started to turn her head away from me, like she was preparing herself for me to say she was a burden and I didn't want her. Well, fuck that shit. I grabbed her chin, turned her head back over her right shoulder and claimed her mouth. I didn't want her to second guess if I wanted her, or our baby. It would be difficult to navigate, but I was determined to try.

With her back to my chest, and one of my hands on her chin, we made out. We made out like horny teens who couldn't control their hormones. As we kissed, my hands started to wander. One of my hands grabbed her right tit and squeezed, causing her to moan. I know this is dangerous, but she needed release, and I liked knowing there was a chance of us being caught. Hell, we were in a hospital room. River had an IV in her arm, but goddammit she was gonna come on my tongue, here and now. I wanted us to have a good memory of learning about this pregnancy. Okay, maybe I also just wanted to taste her. I got off on bringing women pleasure. I broke away from her mouth and started kissing down her neck. "River," I whispered against her skin, and I could feel the goose bumps that pebbled her skin as I spoke. "River, I want you to be a good girl and do just as I say. When I get up, you're going to lay back on the pillow, spread your legs, and let me feast on you in this hospital room till you're coming all over my tongue." I knew my exhibition kink was gonna get me in trouble one of these days, but oh well. Her coming on my tongue was the only thing I cared about right now. River did as I asked, and I don't know how she did it, but she made this hospital gown look sexy. She chuckled when I told her as much, and shook her head from side to side. I groaned and rubbed my hard on through my pants. Fuck, I loved it when my directions in the bedroom, well I guess hospital room in this case, were followed.

I claimed another hard demanding kiss from River before I made my way down her body. When I finally made it to her spread legs, I was delighted to learn she had no underwear on. Just the hospital gown. Usually I would want to tease her, play her body like an instrument. But right now, all I care about is her coming. I kissed her thighs before going straight for her clit. I am honestly surprised by just how wet she was. I

CHAPTER 21

guess our make out session had us both excited. She moaned quietly from my tongue actions on her clit. I sucked hard on her clit just as I roughly pushed two fingers into her. I was a little worried I was too rough on her, but the moan she let out told me otherwise. I went from sucking her clit to licking it quickly. I worked my fingers quickly, searching for the spot inside her. I could feel her cunt gripping my fingers, and I wished it was my dick. But I had enough common sense to realize that was a bad idea. I continued to devour her, her flavor coating my tongue, and I could only hope Raven and I would be able to turn her into a puddle together at some point. The idea of Raven and I working together to bring River to ruin had me moaning, which I guess felt good on River's clit, based on the little gasp she made. Her hand was on my head, pulling me closer to her clit. I knew she was close and I was gonna get her there quickly. I heard footsteps approaching and doubled my efforts, going back to sucking hard. Just as there was a knock on the door, she moaned out my name and came on my tongue. I continued to suck on her till I heard the door start to open. I pulled her gown down, covering her again and sat on the bed, trying to look like I was just sitting by her feet and talking. The knowing smirk on whoever just walked in, told me that we were unable to successfully hide what we were doing in here.

Chapter 22

River

I was shocked. I.... I just let Zane go down on me. In a hospital. The hospital where my father-in-law worked?! What had gotten into me? First, sleeping with Zane at his shop, now letting him go down on me in my hospital bed. I didn't know where the confidence came from, but I kinda liked it. I knew I liked him telling me what to do, and I kinda liked the idea of getting caught. When I heard footsteps coming, it sent me over the edge. I knew I should be paying more attention to whichever medical staff was currently talking to me, but I couldn't bring myself to come back from my happy bubble. I heard Zane talking and knew he was making up for how spacey I was acting right now. Suddenly, there was a hand gripping mine and I heard Zane softly calling my name. I looked up at him and smiled, giving a soft hum to signal to him without words that I was listening. Zane squeezed my hand and told me the tech was here to draw some blood. I nodded but was quickly distracted when I saw that Zane had turned his sweats into a tent. I truly wished we were somewhere where we could fuck. But we were not and as I moved, I realized my body wasn't up to that. But knowing Zane got hard off my pleasure was so very hot. Once the tech took my blood, I was informed that I would

CHAPTER 22

be taken for an ultrasound shortly and then they left.

Once we were alone, I motioned with my finger for Zane to come to me. He did as asked before leaning down and taking my mouth in another demanding kiss. I pulled away, getting ready to tell him what I wanted. He gave me a questioning look and for a moment, I was too embarrassed to ask for what I wanted, but I quickly shook those feelings away. Those were the old River's thoughts. I was the new and improved River and I asked for what I wanted and took it if possible. Between kisses, I whispered my desires to Zane. "I want to watch you stroke yourself till you come, and when you're about to come, I want your cock in my mouth so I get every drop of your cum." I heard Zane moan and I knew he was going to give me what I wanted. I found myself smirking and excited. Obviously he couldn't mouth fuck me because of the concussion, but I want his come.

Zane pulled down his joggers, showing me his impressive length. I didn't really think cocks were nice to look at, but his cock was truly something. I watched as his large, tattooed hand made its way to my cunt. He covered his hand in my juices and started to work himself. All I could hear in the room were our heavy breaths and random noises from the machines. I watched, fixated, as Zane stroked himself. Every couple of strokes, he squeezed the head. He must have been close because he moved. "River, open that pretty mouth. I'm ready to fill it with my cum. Then I want you to leave your mouth open, like the good slut you are. I'm gonna take a picture of that mouth full of my cum. And only when I give my good girl permission, are you allowed to swallow." I did as I was told and opened my mouth, ready to please him. I could feel Zane coming, the warm and slightly salty fluid, filling my mouth. Once he had finished, he pulled away and doing as I was asked, I closed my eyes and opened my mouth. "Good girl, River. Now I want a picture with your mouth and eyes open. I want to be mesmerized every time I look at these pictures, with your eyes calling to me." I opened my eyes, Zane took his pictures, and then told me to swallow. I did. In a raspy voice he says, "Good Girl". Then the tears start. Zane was gonna think I was broken; a complete idiot, with how many times I had cried in front of him. Hell, this was only our third meeting. I had fooled around with him two of those three times, and cried the last two times. And I cried in front of him twice today. Fuck, I was a mess.

Chapter 23

Zane

Why the fuck was she crying again?! Had I pushed her too far? Fuck, she was in a car accident today, was yelled at by the dad of the guy who traumatized her, and learned she was pregnant. Why had I thought she was up for all of what we did? I rushed to her side, pulled her into my arms, and gave her the comfort she deserved. I held her close, sitting on the edge of her bed, and laid her head on my chest while my hands played with her hair. I could already tell she loved having her hair played with. Through her tears River apologized, telling me she was sorry for being such a broken idiot in front of me. I was completely taken off guard. That's not at all what I expected her to say and couldn't have been more wrong. "River," I said, as I continued to play with her hair. "You have done nothing wrong. You have had a roller coaster of a day. I am sorry if I pushed you too far." River immediately shook her head, obviously telling me that I had the wrong idea. She opened her mouth, then paused, seemingly trying to find the right words to say. "Zane, no one has ever told me they've been mesmerized by any part of me before. Also, the praise you offer up, does something to me. I.... I'm still learning what I like and that I have value over being a verbal punching bag that cooks and cleans." After another deep breath, she continued. I was captivated by this woman, who had fought off so many demons and kept on pushing. I don't know how she keeps going, but I want to be there to help her. I want to be there for the ups, the downs, and so much more. "I can't believe anyone would be mesmerized by me. I am fat, make very little money, and have so much trauma I could fill a garbage truck. I do not understand how anyone could see past that. I don't know what's in the future for us, but I will raise our child to have more self worth than I have."

It took me a few moments to respond, as I wanted to ensure I used the right words. I wanted to convey everything I was feeling and be honest, for everyone's sake. "River, I don't know what the future holds for us. I know I want to be there for your good days and bad days. I want to be by your side during this pregnancy. I would love to grow into a relationship. It will be difficult and complicated. I have Raven and our parents to think of. You have a lot of trauma and hurdles to overcome." I can already see her getting ready to pull away, so I quickly continue. "Despite those obstacles, I plan to completely give this my all and I will be there for our child. I have no problem helping you through your traumas. In fact, I would be honored to hold your hand through this hurricane we call life." She gave me a soft smile, and we sat like that for a few more minutes.

"Shit," I cursed, startling River. When she gave me a questioning look, I gave her a half smile and explained. "I forgot to tell Raven and Dakota that they were safe to come back. As long as you're okay with that?" She nodded and laid her head back on my chest, relaxing into me. I could tell she was exhausted, so I stroked her hair while we watched some basic HGTV show, though, I don't think either one of us is actually watching it. We were sitting like that for a little while when there was a knock

CHAPTER 23

at the door. River called to whomever it was, to come in. As the door opened, my eyes met Raven's. She took in how River was cuddled into me and I could see a small smile forming on her lips. The small smile she gave me had me relaxing a bit more. I could tell that she understood and was happy for me. I knew we'd have a lot to talk about later, and a lot to overcome, but we had this. We were stronger together.

We sat in River's room as a group, with HGTV playing in the background and I couldn't help but feel like everything was right at this moment. Like we were all meant to be in each other's lives and it was a powerful feeling.

Once we had been sitting there quietly for about 20 minutes, I heard a snore. Not a soft dainty snore. No, the kind of snore people would typically laugh at in a movie. As funny as that snore was, the sound of it made me relax a little more. She was getting some much needed sleep. As much as I wanted to see our baby, I hoped the ultrasound tech did not come soon, so she could rest.

Chapter 24

Raven

River had been snoring and drooling on Zane's chest for 10 minutes, when I decided she was out enough to talk quietly. I didn't want to hide anything from her, but I also didn't want to overwhelm her. I knew Zane and I would have to have a deeper conversation about what this meant for us, but that conversation was just for us. As quietly as I could, but still loud enough for him to hear, I called his name. He turned to me and we gave each other a smile, finding comfort in our bond. "How is she? Any news?" I asked, knowing that there probably wasn't anything new, but hoping. Zane gently shrugged, conveying 'kinda' pretty well. When he spoke it was in a tone as low as mine. "Not really, we're waiting on an ultrasound. That doctor was escorted out by security and they drew some more blood, I guess for more testing. I don't know when the ultrasound will happen, but I hope it's after she's rested. She had no idea that she was pregnant. She found out at the same time that we did and I hate that man for taking that from her."

Dakota and I sat quietly with those words. I couldn't imagine finding out you're pregnant in such a callus, cruel manner. My heart broke a little for her. We sat there quietly after that, HGTV

CHAPTER 24

playing in the background, just taking in how much our lives changed today.

About an hour later, there was a knock on the door and a short person in blue scrubs walked in. We all looked at them and waited to see what they were there for. "I hope you are all well," they said as their eyes scanned around the room. When they saw Dakota, a huge smile took over their face. Loudly, they said "Dakota", and it startled River awake. I could see by Zane's face that he wanted to deck the tech for being so careless. The tech's face took on a sheepish expression and they apologized before introducing them-self as Joseph and telling us they were there to take River for her ultrasound.

I hated that Dakota and I were going to have to sit in this room and wait, but I knew there was no way we'd all be allowed to go, as we weren't immediate family members.

Panic filled River's eyes, obviously thinking she'd face this alone. That had me wondering how much of her adult life she had faced alone. Sometimes, when she wasn't trying to hide her shadows, I could see through her eyes the demons that haunted her.

Zane grabbed her hand and I could see him give it a tight squeeze, offering comfort to her. "I'm coming with you, River. Don't panic. It's not like I'd let you see our baby for the first time without me." He winked at her and she chuckled, offering him a quick thanks. The tech wheeled her out of the room, Zane walking next to her. He stopped by me and gave me a hug and a kiss on my cheek, assuring me they'd be back soon.

His comforting gesture for her had me filled with panic. I knew it was a completely unreasonable panic, but all the "what ifs" were suddenly filling my head. What if she wasn't actually okay with sharing? What if he picked her over me? What if he got everything we had ever wanted with her, and I was left empty. I knew he took the time to assure me he was coming back, but my brain and intrusive thoughts were in control right now.

I took a few deep breaths and put my elbows on my knees, letting my head fall. I felt a comforting rub on my back, and I knew Dakota was going to be there to help me process all of these messy feelings. "Raven" they said, while still rubbing my back, "talk to me". I took in a deep breath, finding the words that were jumbled in my brain. I finally settled on the two that were taking up the most space, "what if?" They gave me a questioning look, telling me to go on. "All the 'what ifs' are running through my brain. I know there is no logical reason for them. They're my insecurities taking hold of the uncertainty that tonight became and not letting go. But I can't help thinking I'll end up as yesterday's trash, while also knowing that's total bullshit. Zane and I are rock solid, and I don't get bad vibes from River. My brain is just being mean to me." Dakota nodded their head, clearly thinking over what I said. They were quiet for a minute before responding.

"Raven, I think those feelings are valid and for you to belittle your own feelings, minimize them. Feel how you feel, accept them and work through them. I know that's easier said than done though. Zane loves you. Tonight has been a roller coaster and it can't be easy suddenly learning your partner in life is gonna father someone else's baby, but it honestly feels right to me. I can't explain my feelings, they're just there, ya know?"

I nod, because I did know. As hectic as tonight had been and as mean as my thoughts had been, a part of me was sure we were meant to be here. None of us were religious, but sometimes

CHAPTER 24

things just felt right. And as much as I hated the uncertainty, something about this did feel right. I stood up and surprised Dakota with a hug. After that, we went back to sitting in a comfortable silence watching TV, while waiting for Zane and River to come back.

Chapter 25

River

I couldn't wait to be out of this fucking hospital; out of this uncomfortable bed. Out of this overstimulating environment and back home, cuddled up with my mutts. Being rolled through these hallways on this fucking bed had me feeling like I was gonna be sick. Every time they wheeled me from one room to another, I had to close my eyes tightly, and breathe deeply to fight off the nausea. I could hear Zane talking to the tech, but I had no idea what they were talking about. I was too determined to make sure I was not going to be violently ill, rather than pay attention to what they were saying.

Finally, we came to another dull hospital room, with another old ass TV with, you guessed it, HGTV on. Apart from the TV, there was a large computer monitor with two wands next to it. One of the wands looked like the ultrasound device you think of when you think of an ultrasound. The other one made me groan loudly when I realized what it was, the transvaginal ultrasound. I'd had two of them with my annual obgyn appointments, to confirm my PCOS. I hated them, as they always made me feel like I was going to pee myself. I mentally started preparing to have that cold ass wand shoved into my vagina.

As the tech got the bed set up in the new room, they informed

CHAPTER 25

me that the ultrasound tech would be in shortly. I nodded that I understood and thanked them for rolling me around. Through this bland, sick smelling building, though I didn't say it like that, but I sure as hell was thinking it. I waited, and waited some more. That was really all a hospital was. Waiting for something uncomfortable to happen. Eventually Zane walked in from talking to the tech and I gave him a questioning look, but he shook his head and I took that to mean he'd tell me later. Behind Zane was an elderly white lady who smiled at me kindly.

She introduced herself as Karen, and I fought a smirk; an old white lady named Karen, would she live up to her name? Karen went on to explain that she'd be doing my ultrasound. When I nodded to confirm I heard her, she continued. She asked if I had ever had an internal ultrasound before, and I confirmed that I had. The confirmation caused both Zane and Karen to look at me with raised eyebrows. Honestly, if I wasn't so exhausted right now, I would laugh at how comical they looked.

I took a deep breath to prepare myself, as I hated talking about my chronic illnesses. It always made me feel like I was an inconvenience. "My OB/GYN has done it twice, to confirm my PCOS and to check on my ovaries". Karen nodded, not needing more information. I could tell Zane had questions, but he didn't ask and I was grateful for that.

Karen went through everything, making sure I knew what to expect, while also preparing Zane. I got into position, she prepared the wand, and Zane just stared. I realized with where he was, at the foot of the bed, that he was about to get an eye full. "Zane, come stand by my head and hold my hand. I would rather not have you see that wand inside of my vagina." He chuckled and did as asked.

While we waited, his thumb was rubbing my left hand in a

comforting manner and I was honestly very grateful. I squeezed his hand, trying to convey how thankful I was that he was here with me. Once Karen had everything prepared, she let us know we were about to begin. After she started, Zane and I just stared at the screen, as if we would immediately see the baby I was carrying. It was at this moment that it hit me. I was aware that I was pregnant, but now it felt fucking real.

I must have zoned out with those thoughts floating through my mind, because suddenly I heard Zane take in a sharp breath. When I came back to myself, I looked at Zane who was looking at the screen and squeezing my hand, and I realized he must be seeing something. Quickly I looked at the screen and took in what I was seeing. There wasn't a lot, but there was a small, sack-like thing, and I just knew that was our baby. *Our baby*!

Chapter 26

Zane

After getting to see the little sack on the screen, I knew that was our fetus. I didn't have words. Today had thrown off my entire life plan, but I would have been lying if I said I wasn't excited to see where this took us. I had always wanted kids, I just wanted it to be at the right time. I'd have to make now the right time. I had a lot going on in my life, but I was a determined fucker and would make this happen. I'd make sure it happened in the best way possible for everyone . Karen left River and I alone, and for a minute we just stared. I was still holding her hand as we gazed at the image of our fetus, that would slowly grow into our child.

Our child.

I turned to look at River, ready for whatever was to come. She was still staring, shock written all over her face, at the picture of the sack. Our fetus. I squeezed her hand and she looked over at me with a small smile on her face, and it was then I realized, we were in this. We were gonna make our child's life the best we possibly could. No, matter what was to come.

Once we were back in River's room she turned to me, and I could see tears in her eyes. The panic immediately set in. I had been so excited, I hadn't even stopped to consider how this was going to impact River. The guilt I was hit with was suddenly overwhelming. How could I have been such a selfish asshat? Both of our lives had just changed so drastically but River's life had done absolutely nothing but change over the last few years.

I guess she could read the emotions written all over my face because she tried to hide her face from me. But that was not how I wanted to start this journey together. We may not know each other well but her soul calls to mine, and I can tell she always puts others, and their feelings, before anything for herself.

Using my right hand I grabbed her chin, with my thumb under her lips, and pulled her face back to mine. I followed my instincts, holding eye contact, silently letting her know I was here for what she needed. Eventually she relaxed, closed her eyes and I saw more tears fall. Leaning forward, I let go of her chin, and pulled her in for a hug and slowly kissed away her salty tears. We sat like that for several minutes until we were no longer alone. As I moved away to make room for the medical professionals, I leaned in and whispered in her ear "We will work this out. I am here for you. You will be mine and I will be yours." When her cheeks began to flush pink, I leaned in, and dropped a fast peck to her lips, cementing that statement for the world to see. Well, maybe not the world, but the few people in this room and whatever is in the universe.

River was rolled back up to her room with me following behind, giving us both a moment to feel everything and consider what we each wanted. The hospital wasn't the place for this talk. Add in the recent traumatic events and now was definitely not the time, but I knew it was coming soon.

After hours of being in this brand, HGTV filled the hospital, River was finally sent home. I was in the room when the doctor

CHAPTER 26

cleared her from the wreck and asked her to stay home and rest. She was also instructed to get some prenatal vitamins and asked to schedule an appointment with her OB/GYN. I didn't miss her wince when her OB/GYN was mentioned, and I had to wonder what the cause of that wince was. As I was contemplating that, a sudden look of complete relief took over Rivers's face and I heard her say "Fee".

I was only confused for a moment, before a short white man walked over and gave River a huge hug. The grip she had on him sparked little flames of jealousy within, which I pushed down. As much as I wanted to rip her from his arms, my rational brain was telling me she needed his comfort. So I stomped my caveman instincts down and took comfort in the fact that she was being comforted. Eventually she pulled away, with a slight wince on her pretty face due to the injuries from the wreck, and turned to me with a small smile. "Zane, this is Fe. We've been friends since we were both little girls in Pre-K. He's my best friend." Gesturing at me, she continued "Fe, this is Zane..." She trailed off, obviously unsure how to introduce me. Eventually she settled on, "Remember the tattoo artist I told you about?"

I don't miss the moment of shock that crosses Fe's face. He turned to me with a huge smile. "I have heard wonderful things and the tattoo you did is amazing. I am so glad to meet you and see you here. River has been confusing the fuck out of me when it comes to you." I blinked at Fe, shocked that River had been talking about me. I heard a groan from behind Fe and chuckled as I met River's wide eyes. Now I knew she'd been talking about me to her best friend and that knowledge brought me some form of comfort. We talked for a moment longer, and River told Fe she'd explain everything as soon as we were all out of the "HGTV hell". The HGTV slander earned chuckles from both Fe and I. I walked them both to Fe's car, ensuring River made it to the car without further injury. Once River was seated safely in Fe's passenger seat, I gave her a kiss on the forehead and asked for a text when they made it safely home. She gave me a small, shy smile and promised the text.

Once I watched them pull away, I called Raven. I wasn't entirely sure where she and Dakota ended up. It rang twice before she answered with a giggle and said "hellllooo lover boy." I groaned; wine, right. I asked where they were and she said they stepped outside for some fresh air, so we made plans to meet at the car.

When I finally got to the car, I was immediately comforted by the sight of Raven and Dakota. As soon as I was close enough, I grabbed Raven and hugged her tightly. She was my comfort. My rock. My best friend. My lover. And I knew I needed her comfort now more than ever. Today has been one hell of a day. She hugged me back, no words passing between us as they weren't needed. No matter what happened, we'd get through this together.

The drive home was quiet, soft music playing in the background, but no words passing between us. Everyone was tired and deep in their own thoughts. When we made it home, Dakota made their way to their room, with a quick goodnight and hugs. Raven and I slowly made it to our en-suite where we slowly kissed each other, taking comfort in the familiarity of each other's kisses. We slowly started stripping off our clothes as we kissed. I pulled away for a moment to turn on the shower, and when I turned back around I took a moment to stare at this stunning woman, who I somehow got to claim as mine. Her dark skin reflected the light beautifully. Her tits were a perfect handful, with hard,

CHAPTER 26

dark nipples, just begging for my mouth. As my gaze traveled her body, I noted the dark hair between her legs, knowing I am about to taste one of my favorite flavors in the world.

Before I got to devouring her, I went to my knees in front of her. I just wanted this hug. I pulled her close and laid my head on her soft belly. "You're beautiful. I can never fully tell you how much you mean to me. Thank you for being here for me. Thank you, for everything." With those words, I started peppering her body with small soft kisses. She didn't respond to my words, but she didn't need to. Her soft, quiet moans filled the bathroom. Tonight wasn't about kinky, wild sex. Tonight I was gonna make love to this beautiful woman who I never wanted to let go.

Her moans grew louder as I made my way up her stomach, standing so I could kiss her lips again. Once I was up and devouring her mouth, our tongues dancing in familiarity that brought comfort and soft moans, I lifted her and she wrapped her strong legs around my hips. Her wet core ground into my hard length and she whimpered, needing relief and desperately searching for friction. That wouldn't do. I planned on making her come undone on my tongue. I wanted Dakota to be able to hear me make her scream from their bedroom. I set her on the counter and spread her legs, looking at her glistening pussy lips. The dark color of them, covered in her wetness, had me licking my lips.

I planned on enjoying every moment of this. Slowly, I started kissing her left ankle, running my tongue over the small scar she had there. I could feel her shudder as I placed kisses slowly up her leg. Once I made it to the apex of her thighs, I placed a small gentle kiss before giving her right leg the same treatment. As Raven trembled from anticipation, I spread her pussy lips and licked long and slow. I groaned, her tasting like home. I devoured her, teasing and tasting. Once I could tell she was on the edge, I started sucking her clit, circling it with my tongue. As I tasted and teased, I slowly worked two fingers inside her, stretching and adding to her sensation. I felt her clench on my fingers, and I could tell she was close. I sucked hard on her clit, and refused to let up, as she screamed and then relaxed against the mirror, worn out. I teased her a little longer, enjoying sending shocks through her body. "Zane," she said softly, and I pulled away, looking up at the bliss on her face from my knees. I knew when she said my name in that manner, that she was overstimulated and ready for a break from her clit. Slowly I kissed both of her thighs again before standing.

I pulled her to the edge of the counter and guided her legs back around my middle. We both watched as my length entered her wet center and moaned in satisfaction. We stayed like that for a moment. Just taking comfort in each other. Slowly I started rocking my hips. We kissed deeply and I steadily rocked in and out of her, her tight heat gripping me. Our moans filled the bathroom, the steam from the shower falling around us like our own private cloud. We slowly moved together 'til I filled her and then kissed her deeply. We stayed locked together and I pulled my lips away, to put my forehead to hers. Breathing deeply I whispered, "I love you, Raven. I can never tell you that enough."

With those words I carried her into the shower before putting her down and holding her close as she stood under the hot spray. We kissed passionately for a moment, before washing quickly.

Once we were clean, we got out of the shower, brushed our teeth, and got in bed. I held her tightly and thought about the day. Her scent and soft breaths helped me fall into a deep sleep.

CHAPTER 26

My happy place was holding Raven as we fell asleep, but part of me couldn't help but wonder if we could possibly add a third to this happy place.

Chapter 27

River

Today had been one hell of a day, but I was going to be thankful for the small things and just be glad I did not have to stay overnight. The hospital originally said I would need to and if there is a God, maybe they heard my pleas and sent me home. Though somehow I ended up having an extra being inside of me, so I guess I really needed to process that. Luckily Fe was here and he was amazing at listening and processing. I truly believed Fe might be the best person on this planet.

The ride home was quiet, Spotify playing music from the nineties in the background, allowing me to gather my thoughts and figure out what I wanted to say to Fe. When we pulled up to my childhood home about 20 minutes later, I just sat and stared. It was so weird to think my childhood home could be the same home for my child. My life had not been anything like I planned, but that's what's wrong with planning I guess. As a kid, I wanted to be a stay at home mom with three kids, by the time I was 30. Now, I couldn't imagine not working. Never in my life plan did I think I'd be a widow in my 30's and pregnant for the first time by a man I didn't really know. What a life, I guess?

CHAPTER 27

I suppose I was in my head for too long because I heard Fe call my name. "River? Are you ready?" I nodded and cleared my head. I needed to go assure my parents I was okay, tell them we'd talk tomorrow, and then talk to Fe while I cuddled with the mutts. We made our way inside, checking to make sure my parents' dogs were up and let mine out into the back yard to let them do their business. While Fe went to the bathroom, I went and searched for my parents. I found my dad in the living room watching the news. When he saw me, I could see the relief on his face. I had done nothing but make their lives so stressful over the last year and a half, and I felt awful. Taking a deep breath, I voiced, "Hey dad. Where's mom?" I'm sure she was in bed with a migraine; I got my chronic migraines from her. When he confirmed my suspicion, I let out the breath I was holding. I'm just so glad I get to sleep on my feelings, as my mom would have so many questions. I nodded and continued, "I'm okay dad. Just really tired. Fe is gonna stay tonight and watch over me. Can we talk tomorrow and I'll explain everything to y'all?"

I could tell he was searching for whatever I was not saying. But I knew my dad wouldn't push, he'd wait and be the most supportive person. For the first time since the crash, I felt true relief. My parents would be the best grandparents. At this moment, I decided I wouldn't tell them that part tomorrow, but wait and give them the cutest pregnancy announcement. With that thought, I finally felt excited. I wasn't an idiot. It would be hard as hell and stressful, but worth it. I gave my dad the biggest hug, told him I loved him and left to get Fe and my mutts.

When the mutts' water bowl had been refilled, Fe and I each had a bottle of water (God what I wouldn't give for a Coke Zero right now), we laid down on my couch to talk. The dogs were spread out around the room, chewing on toys, and relaxing without a care in the world. I was petting Roddy, trying to figure out where to start. Finally, I started with the worst possible way to fucking start. "So, today I learned I'm pregnant." I guess I should have waited for Fe to drink his water, because suddenly the water he had been about to swallow was all over poor Roddy, and Fe was coughing like he was drowning. "Oops, I guess I should have waited to tell you that part." Fe just looks at me before talking. "*You think*?! River, I'm going to need you to start from the beginning. But you are going to be the absolute best mom."

And with that, I let out the whole story. I talked about how when I got my tattoo, I was finally comfortable with someone and needed a new touch. How I only planned on a kiss, but we kept going. How wonderful Zane was and how he made sure to have consent from both me and Raven at every step of the way. Then I went on to explain how I pulled away and let my insecurities get to me. How the feelings from my marriage stopped me from pursuing what I wanted and how I didn't want to be a burden on anyone else's life. I explained just how much I have felt like I keep ruining peoples lives and how I did not want to bring that on people as wonderful as Zane and Raven. From there, I talked about therapy today and how I had finally decided to do something for myself. How I ultimately had texted Zane, which ended with me being hit and ending up in the hospital.

I took a deep breath before continuing. I told Fe about how Zane showed up at the hospital and was there for me. Then I had to tell him about the encounter with my previous father-in-law. I told Fe how awful it was to learn about the pregnancy in that manner and how I hated that Zane learned that way as well. I ended my story by pulling out my phone and showing Fe the

CHAPTER 27

photo of my ultrasound. It was all too much. I was tired, I hurt, was so mentally drained, and hadn't yet had time to process anything. I was suddenly crying in Fe's arms, forever grateful for my best friend. Eventually, we made our way to bed where we talked about everything and Fe made sure to tell me how I was the furthest thing from a burden. Before I fell asleep, I pulled my phone out and sent Zane a quick text.

River: Goodnight, I can't believe we made this. I hope you sleep well, we'll talk soon. Thank you for your support.

I was taken aback when I got a response from Zane. He "loved" the picture, then told me goodnight and to sleep well.

I must have slept for twelve hours. My body was so sore and tired. I knew it needed to recover and the bean inside me also needed me to rest and get back on my feet. I still couldn't get over how crazy it was that I was pregnant. I was on the bed, surrounded by my mutts, and content when I became suddenly nauseated. I was up and running to the bathroom, emptying my already empty stomach, before sitting back on my heels. I took a moment and thought, and that's when I realized I had been feeling more sick than normal recently. I thought it was my PTSD and chronic illness, but I bet it was morning sickness. I got up off the floor, washed out my mouth, brushed my teeth, and went on the hunt for my parents.

Luckily, they were both taking lunch and working at home. Fe left this morning while I was still asleep, but he sent me a text telling me he loved me and he'd be there for me for everything. I cried when I read it and fell back asleep. My dogs were outside, and I wished I had their comfort right now. I knew my mom was going to panic when she saw my body. I had avoided looking in mirrors since the wreck for the same reason. I heard a sharp intake of breath as I sat, and looked up to meet my mom's eyes. I could see the fear there. I grabbed her hand and assured her that I was okay. I told them about therapy and that I thought I made progress, but how I ended up getting hit by another driver while going to get a Coke Zero. I made sure they knew I was mostly just covered in small cuts and bruises. I did have a possible concussion and one broken wrist, but luckily it was my left arm so I could still function. I continued, telling them I was given a week off work, just to start, and that I would call my insurance and a lawyer this week. Since it was a big rig that hit me, and they were in the wrong, they might settle and give me enough to cover bills and get a new vehicle. They listened and gave me big hugs, confirming that they would help me in every possible way. With that, I told them I wanted to rest and went to grab the dogs. That way we could all comfort watch Good Mythical Morning on YouTube and zone out. Just what I needed after the last 24 hours.

Chapter 28

Raven

My body was still hot with the remembered words and touches with Zane last night. I was always amazed at how he could still bring me to that place, even after so long together. I felt so special that I was still his comfort place and I knew that would never change. The look Dakota had given me when they left this morning said they had heard my moans and screams last night. I had just shrugged. What did I have to be ashamed of? I had a man that knew how to make me come and had the best cock I had ever ridden.

Thinking of Zane and last night had me wanting to show him I was going to support him through this journey. I knew he really liked River and wanted to make things work with her, especially now that he was gonna be a daddy. Zane was at the shop today, on his day off, to finish a special tattoo. I was off today and wanted to take our different days off to show him I was gonna support him. Earlier, I had borrowed his phone to get River's phone number without telling him. I wanted it to be a surprise that I reached out to her. I was so happy to see that they had sent each other goodnight and good morning texts, and some general conversation texts. I truly hoped those were good signs, but I hadn't read anymore. It wasn't my business and I trusted Zane.

With Zane gone, I pulled out my phone to send him a quick "have a good day and love you" text, before pulling up the newly added contact-River. I stared at it for a few seconds, before doing what I wanted to and sending her a text.

Raven: Hey! This is Raven. Zane's at work today and I was wondering if I could take you out? I want to get to know you better and I'm starving.

I was pleasantly surprised when I got a text back, immediately.

River: Hey! I would love that. Are leggings and a shirt okay? I am too beat up from yesterday for more. But I really want to get to know you too, you're beautiful and seem like a truly amazing person.

She surprised me again by being so forward. With how she originally ghosted Zane, I expected her to pull away from me, but I was glad she wasn't. With a few more texts, we made plans for me to get her in an hour. I spent the next 45 minutes getting ready and watching the food network. I had on leggings and a shop t-shirt, my comfort outfit, but I wanted to make sure River knew I didn't care what she was wearing. I also only put on light mascara. Today wasn't about impressing anyone, but actually getting to know one another. With 15 minutes to go, I hopped in my Rav-4 and headed over to pick up River. She had sent me her address earlier when we confirmed the time, and I asked her not to tell Zane I texted her. She was worried about that request, since they're really just starting out, but I assured her I had a good reason.

CHAPTER 28

When I pulled up to her house, I saw River sitting on the front porch talking to the middle aged white man we met last night at the hospital. I was pretty sure she said he was her dad, but I couldn't remember a name. Something about him reminded me of my dad and my instincts told me they'd be trouble together.

River must have seen me pull up, because she stood and started walking to the car. I saw her flip the bird at her dad as she walked away and they both laughed. I was shocked because I have never shot the bird at my parents. When she got to the car, I could see the laughter on her face and found that I wanted to be a part of their joy. I was drawn into their energy like a bee to a flower.

When she got in the car, we greeted each other and sat in an awkward silence for a moment. I mean why wouldn't it be awkward? We learned last night she was pregnant by my boyfriend, who is also my step brother. God, that's such a weird sentence that just went through my brain. I chuckled at my internal thoughts and she looked at me with a question on her face. It caused me to crack up even more. Through laughs that make me want to pee myself, I explained. "I was just thinking why didn't I expect the awkward silence? I mean, last night, in an insanely traumatic way, we learned you're pregnant by my boyfriend, who is also my step brother?! Which is a weird ass sentence and it started my laughter. But why did I not expect the awkward silence. I mean, it should be awkward."

My word salad sent River into hysterical laughter too and she said "OMG, don't make me laugh so hard. My ribs. God, our situation sounds like something out of a romance author's mind." After we both calmed down, she told me she had a real craving for the Awful Waffle and off we went. Our first date was gonna be amazing.

When we got to the restaurant with its bright yellow name, I heard River's stomach growl. She held her arm, the one in a cast, to her stomach and looked sheepish. Eventually she told me she hadn't really eaten. We made our way inside and she started to order a Coke Zero before catching herself and ordering a Sprite. When I shot her a questioning glance, she shrugged and said, "I did some basic googling and caffeine and pregnancy is a no go..." I could tell she wanted to say more, so I waited, knowing eventually she'd continue.

After a few moments she finally started to talk, but it was shy and I got the feeling she was holding back tears. "Raven, I just want to say I am sorry. I pulled away from Zane because I constantly feel like I am a burden on others, and I did not want to become a burden on y'all." She took a deep breath and continued before I could tell her she didn't owe me an apology. "In the end, it appears I am adding a burden to y'all's lives anyways. Even if we don't end up together, I am bringing a new life into this world, and it's part of Zane. I want you to know I will never come between you and Zane. I really like both of y'all, but I will pull away before I can negatively impact either of you. I am sure I could have worded that better, but I just wanted you to know I will follow y'all's lead, but I do think taking it slow is best."

"River, I do not blame you for anything. I am so excited to be with you on this journey. I do think you should apologize to Zane for pulling away, but I know you will. This baby is going to be beautiful and my gut tells me the three of us will end up together. But I agree that taking it slow is best."

I think our waitress knew whatever we were talking about was serious, because she dropped our drinks off without saying a word. River picked up her Sprite and took a huge sip while

CHAPTER 28

she blinked quickly. I could guess she was blinking back the tears I could see forming in her eyes. After her sip, she cussed under her breath and murmured about forgetting to say no ice. I kept that information in the back of my mind, River is a no ice girly. River ordered a chicken melt, no bacon, no pickles, hash browns with onions and cheese, and a waffle. I did the all star breakfast, do my hash browns the same way as River, sunny side up egg, and apple butter with my toast.

Our meal was amazing. The Awful Waffle never disappointed with food. River and I talked, getting to know each other on a basic level. We talked about pets, books, food, tattoos, piercings, and so much more. It was clear to me that we had so much in common. We joked about how Zane found two girls with similar names and all the same loves, and how two book girlies would get expensive. Eventually we finished our meal, talking about how stuffed we were, and headed back to my car.

Once we were in the car, we decided to keep the date going and head over to Target and Marshalls. I mean, where else would we go? River and I had a fantastic time shopping. We looked at books, underwear, the sex toys that Target now sells, makeup, and eventually baby stuff. When we got to the baby section, I could tell River was going back into her head again. We walked around and she poked at a few things, but didn't pick anything up. It seemed strange to me, so I put a few gender neutral items in the cart. River looked truly surprised and I just smiled and hugged her.

"Raven," she said in a quiet voice. "I am still very early. I don't know if we should buy anything. I could very easily miscarry. I have a lot of health issues and severe PTSD and anxiety. All of that can negatively impact the pregnancy. Maybe we just get prenatal vitamins for now? The idea of spending money on stuff and then having to donate it or return it breaks my heart. I don't know if my heart can handle it. The man that left me a widow did so much damage, it's hard to put into words just how scared I am. Letting you and Zane in. This baby. I could lose it all again and be left even more broken than I already am."

I was taken back. I knew she was excited for this baby, but I could never imagine feeling the pain that filled her voice. The constant worry about opening yourself back up and having it ripped away from you, must be exhausting. Her emotions must be in a constant turmoil and I could see that all over her face. I could see her trying to put herself back together, working to put a smile on to cover her pain. I could see just how much she put on to keep others comfortable.

I guess I was quiet too long because she started talking again. "I didn't mean to dump all of that on you. I am sorry Raven. I just want to be realistic and see a doctor. You don't need to know about the inner workings of my mind, especially on our first date. I'm gonna go grab the vitamins and then we can go." Before I could respond, she was off. I decided I was still going to get the few things I picked out as they weren't big. Just some toys and gender neutral outfits. I headed to the front and checked out. While I waited for River, I came up with a plan. I knew she probably wanted to go home and cry, but I wanted to bring her to my sanctuary. I wanted to show her that no matter what happened, she wasn't alone.

Chapter 29

River

God, I was such a fucking mess. I couldn't believe I dumped all of that on her in the middle of the God damn baby section of Target. She just wanted to do something sweet. While I knew my concerns were based a lot on my trauma, I was also very much aware that the chance of a miscarriage was very much real. I just wished I had worded everything differently. Staring at the vitamin section, I got even more frustrated. Why were there so many fucking vitamin choices?! How was I supposed to know which is best?! Eventually, I googled the best and picked the ones Google recommended to me, before heading to the front of the store to check out.

When I got there, I found Raven already done with her purchases, so I couldn't tell if she actually bought the baby stuff. I am pretty sure she probably did. My trauma didn't mean she and Zane couldn't get stuff. Once I checked out, I walked over to her and apologized again. "Raven, I am sorry. My trauma doesn't mean you and Zane cannot enjoy this. I want the two of you to experience all the happiest parts of this." She smiled and hugged me, telling me she understood and didn't blame me. We walked to her car, got in, and she started driving. I fully expected her to take me home after my spectacular breakdown, but she started driving in the other direction.

Before I could ask her where we were going she said, "I wanna take you to one of my happy places. I go here whenever I need time to think. It's about an hour away, so it will be dark by the time we get there but I think we could both use the serenity that comes with this place." I nodded and settled into the seat. I was exhausted and the soft sounds of the music eventually led me into a soft sleep.

I guess I slept for the entire drive, because I felt my shoulder being gently rocked and heard my name being said in a soft tone. I slowly came to and wiped the drool from my cheek. I blushed. God, I am so embarrassed! Raven only laughed and dropped a soft kiss to my lips. I was so surprised that she was out of the car before I could kiss her back. As I opened the car door, I touched my lips and could feel the butterflies in my stomach going crazy for a good reason.

I didn't know what I expected when I got out of the car, but it wasn't a church. I was raised in a really relaxed church, but I really didn't care for organized religion; they tend to spread more hate than love. Before I could ask her any questions, Raven said "I'm not a religious person, but this place always makes me feel comfortable. This was the church my grandmother would bring me to as a kid. The beauty of it always puts me at ease." I looked around and realized she was right. The small white building with stained glass was beautiful and something about it felt very welcoming.

We sat on the porch of the church and Raven told me about her childhood here. How she was pretty sure her grandma was sleeping with the wife of the pastor. Her stories made me ache for a childhood church experience I did not get. While

CHAPTER 29

the church I went to was more accepting, I still very much felt uncomfortable and unwelcome. It was clear to me that the pressure of the Bible wasn't forced on her here. It was more about community and love than anything. Raven told me about how she would climb the trees with friends and how she fell out of the tree once and broke her arm. Her grandma had rushed out of the church looking all sorts of undone. She showed me where the Easter egg hunts had been, and talked about all the wonderful people she met there. She went on to say that while it was still beautiful and a peaceful place for her, it was no longer the same church she went to as a kid. It had become filled with hate and bigotry, and she could only come here when it was empty because they didn't approve of her "lifestyle".

After an hour, she finally took me inside and I was taken aback by the beauty of the small building. The small church was quaint and not pretentious in any way. The stained glass was even more beautiful from the inside and I could only imagine how the light looked coming through it. As beautiful as the church was, it was Raven's beauty that really captured me in this moment. Her dark skin shone and peace radiated off her. It was at this moment I decided I wanted to worship at her altar. I wanted to bring her to a place of bliss in this beautiful place. I walked up to her, in this place of worship, and brought her lips to mine. While I identified as Bi, I had never really been with a woman and to say I was nervous, was an understatement. When Raven didn't immediately kiss me back, I panicked and started to pull away. But before I could, she bit my lip and kissed me back hard.

Chapter 30

Raven

I must have drawn blood when I bit River, because I can taste it dancing on our tongues as they move together. I wanted to apologize for the bite, but her moan had me convinced she liked it. The way her moan echoed around the church was intoxicating and had my panties soaking. This kiss was full of passion and God damn was I here for it. This church where families sit and pray, was about to be full of the cries of two women coming together for the first time.

River and I were standing in the front of the church, like we were going to put on a show for our congregation, and it felt like we were doing something dirty and beautifully both wrong and right. River's hands dropped from being wrapped around my middle, to my waist, pulling me closer till our chests were rubbing against each other. My hands were on the hem of her shirt, playing with it and slowly lifting it up. I was a little surprised when River let go of my waist and broke our kiss. I was sure she was about to pull away, but instead she ripped her shirt off, quickly followed by her bralette, and threw them both on the floor. Before I could respond, she turned her back to me, and I was distracted from what she was doing by the sway of her ass.

CHAPTER 30

When she turned back around she had her good hand hidden behind her back and took my hand with the one in a cast. She led me to a pew, keeping one hand hidden, and gently pushed me into the bench while she got on her knees in front of me. I was distracted by whatever she dropped to the ground, by her lips crashing into mine again. While we kissed, my hands wandered over her full and heavy breasts. Her light pink nipples were hard and I ached to kiss them, so I did just that. Her breaths were heavy as I sucked on one nipple and pinched the other one. The moment got to me and I bit the nipple in my mouth, drawing forth her cries and leading her to squeeze her thighs together. Her excitement over the pain had me so excited.

When I pulled away to the other nipple, she grabbed the bottom of my shirt and lifted, leaving me in my lacy, hot pink bra. I loved the way she stared at the bright color against my dark skin. River leaned forward and started kissing down my neck, between my tits, then pulled the cups of my bra down, leaving my nipples exposed. My head fell back in ecstasy as her mouth claimed my right nipple and her hands started moving slowly up my thighs, towards my center. She teased me through my pants and had me ready to beg before she pulled away.

Before I had time to process that she'd moved away, my bra was off and she was tugging at the waistband of my leggings. I lifted my hips and she pulled my leggings and thong down to my ankles. Suddenly, I heard cursing and looked down. River was fighting with my shoes in her rush to get me naked. I let out a small chuckle that turned into a moan when she took my nipple in her mouth again, distracting me from her struggle with my shoes. While she played with my nipples, she won her battle and next thing I knew I was sitting naked in the pews of my childhood church.

Chapter 31

River

R iver
God, I was so fucking nervous. I had this beautiful goddess of a woman sitting naked in front of me, while my soft stomach and floppy arms were on display, but I was not about to let my insecurities ruin this for me. While I had Raven distracted by playing with her perfect tits, I reached behind me and grabbed one of the items I took from the stage of the church. If I was gonna fuck in a church, I was gonna go all out.

I brought the juice used for communion between us and poured the liquid over one of her boobs, before I used my tongue to clean her up. I would have done the wine, but pregnancy meant that wasn't an option, so I was glad when I saw the juice. Raven was definitely shocked, the juice obviously surprising her, but her moans mixing with giggles told me she liked it. Kneeling in front of her wasn't really giving me the best access, so I stood, pulling my leggings off as I did. Raven watched, and surprise filled her gaze when she saw that I didn't have on any underwear. When we were both naked, I gently pushed Raven down so she was laying on the church pew and I was leaning over her.

With her laying down, legs spread, I put my knee between her thighs to give her something to grind on. While she ground

CHAPTER 31

her glistening pussy on my knee, I leaned down and kissed her, hard. I poured more of the juice over her and slowly licked it up, my tongue following the path of the liquid over her body. Eventually the juice brought me face to face with her pussy.

Nerves shot through me and I looked up, finding Raven watching me through half hooded eyes. I spoke before I lost my nerve. "Raven, I'm bi but I have never actually been with another woman. I want you to guide me and tell me exactly what you want." Her voice was full of desire when she responded, "I can do that River. Now be a good girl and lick my pussy and tell me how I taste." Her dirty words and orders had me wishing for my own relief. But I was also so glad she understood and gave me directions. I leaned down and did just as I was told, licking her glistening cunt and groaning at her taste on my tongue. She tasted like the best kind of temptation. When I told her as much, I heard her chuckle, but I stopped that chuckle with another long lick.

Her cunt was quickly becoming my favorite place. I was intoxicated by her smell and taste. Everything just felt so right, like I was supposed to be bringing her to her own heaven in this church. My tongue slowly moved up her slit, till it was circling around her clit. As I pulled my tongue away from her clit and spread her lips with my fingers, I stuck my tongue as deeply into her pussy as I could. Moaning, Raven gave me my next directive, "River, use your fingers to rub my clit while you fuck me with your tongue." She looked beautifully disheveled, gazing down her body to me with my tongue deep inside her cunt. Before I did as I was told, I reached down and grabbed two church wafers. Raven looked confused as she saw them, but I spread her lips and stuck them inside her. She sucked in a deep breath and moaned loudly as I did what I was told. I heard her call me a good girl, as I rubbed circles on her clit and fucked her with my tongue. It wasn't long before she was coming all over my face. I pulled my fingers away and slowly started to lick up her release. Her fingers threaded through my hair and she started to pull my head away.

    I let her pull me away, but not before I used my tongue to get the church wafers from her cunt. I showed them to her, soaked with her release. She watched me stick one on my tongue and eat it. I offered her the second one and Raven stuck her tongue out, moaning as she tasted herself on the wafer. Somehow our debauchery in the church had me feeling so relaxed and at peace. I realized that I didn't even need to finish, I just wanted to sit with this feeling and hold Raven. So, that's exactly what I did. I moved us down so we weren't sitting in the mess we made, and held her. I let myself feel all the confusing emotions and just relaxed into them. I knew this was probably not how anyone pictured today going, but I was so very glad it did.

    We sat like that for a while longer, Raven completely naked in front of me and I could not stop staring. That's when suddenly headlights illuminated the interior of the church as someone pulled into the parking lot. Immediately our little slice of bliss was filled with the panic of two women being caught naked and sticky on this church pew, in this place of worship for who knows how many people. We both jumped up and rushed to get dressed. Raven's bottoms were in the pew, but our shirts were up on the stage. While Raven covered up her bottom half, I rushed to grab out shirts, my tits jumping painfully and comically, but I didn't really have the brain power to worry about that. We rushed getting our clothes thrown on and by the time the doors to the church opened, we looked like we'd been up to no good, but we were fully clothed.

Chapter 32

Zane

I hadn't heard from Raven in hours and I was starting to get worried. She hadn't told me her plan for the day. I assumed she'd enjoy a nice relaxing day at home, but when I wasn't getting the usual random texts and TikTok links, I got nervous. I sent a few texts and got no response, which was so unlike Raven. I also hadn't heard from River and my intrusive thoughts were trying to tell me she was running again, though I was trying not to let them win.

After hours of not hearing anything, I finally decided to check Raven's location. It wasn't something I would normally do, I trusted Raven, but with everything that had happened, I was concerned. What if she panicked and tried to leave? What if she was in a wreck? So many what-ifs were floating through my mind, so I decided to ease my worries by checking her location. Turns out it did not help my concerns. Whenever Raven went to her grandma's church, it was usually because she had something on her mind. So, I decided to head that way.

I got home from the tattoo parlor about an hour ago, showered, and fed the cats, so all I needed to do was throw on some clothes and shoes. I landed on gray sweatpants that I knew Raven loved, a black Butch Walker concert t-shirt, and some slides. Comfortable, fast, and easy, just what I needed to go comfort Raven.

I drove about an hour, with music playing quietly in the background, trying to relax and not worry. I might have sped a little bit, but luckily no cops. When I got to the church, I saw her Rav-4 and parked next to her.

When my headlights lit up the church, I was shocked to see two people. I was pretty sure I could also see the outline of naked boobs? What the actual fuck was happening? I turned my car off, got out, and walked up the stairs to the church. I was greeted by the faces of the two women I'd been thinking of, both Raven and River. They were both so disheveled, I was sure they had been up to no good in this church. I was stunned, shocked, and silent. I truly have no idea what to say.

Before I could pull my jaw up off the floor, Raven spoke. "Fuck, Zane. You made us so worried." She leaned forward and placed a quick kiss on my lips and I was pretty sure I could taste Raven's juices on her lips. Turning to River, I gave her a hug, and she definitely smelled like Raven and sex. What the fuck did I just walk in on? "What is happening? I haven't heard from y'all in hours and I find y'all disheveled in an old church?" The blush that filled River's cheeks was so satisfying; her pale skin showed the rosy color so well. Raven just rolled her eyes and started to walk out. As she walked away, Raven said "Can we go home and talk about what happened?" Before I could protest, River spoke up and said, "Can we go to my house? I need to go home and take care of my mutts and take my meds. Or can I be dropped off before you talk, cause I just realized this conversation wasn't meant for me. Anddddd now I feel like an idiot."

I was shocked when Raven turned to her, placed a kiss on her

CHAPTER 32

lips, and told her to go get in her car. Like the good girl she is, River did as told. When she moved, Raven called her "good girl," just like I was thinking, and the flush deepened. Once River was situated in the car, Raven turned to me and told me to follow her to River's house and that once we talked to her there, the two of us would then talk at our house. With that, we were back on the road and headed to River's home.

I don't know what I expected River's home to be, but it was a charming, two story house. I could tell her parents had lived here awhile, because it definitely needed some help. The exterior was a light green color, with colorful lawn ornaments everywhere. It was charming and didn't really fit into the neatness of the rest of the neighborhood. I liked it; it was comforting and felt like it would be a safe and non-judgmental space. River and Raven got out of the car and I could feel the stress coming off River in waves. Raven and I shared a look and I could hear River taking a deep breath.

"Okay," River started. "After my husband ended his life, I had to move home. I was put in a lurch; please know it's cramped and cluttered. My dogs will be hyper. You might meet my parents and I have not told them about the pregnancy. Please don't judge me. I have never been the best at cleaning." It was so clear to me that she had struggled with this for so long, and she was always worried about what people thought. " River, you don't need to worry about either one of us ever judging you." With my firm statement, I could see her relax some. Seeing the stress leave her shoulders helped me feel more at ease. Backing up, she slowly started to lead us into her home. I could immediately tell that she wasn't lying about the clutter, but that was okay; some people are just like that.

As we entered her living space, I saw three large dogs, who immediately started barking and were excited to greet us. On River's walls there were shelves covered in books, photos of her dogs, and a pride flag that was hanging up next to her bookshelf. The space felt so much like River that I couldn't imagine anyone else living here. River introduced us to the two dogs that weren't in crates first. non-judgmental, who she said was the oldest and her hippo, and Roddy, who was apparently a dog version of a garbage disposal. Then she turned to the loudest barker of them all. Matty-ice was licking me and Roddy was begging Raven for pets, as she introduced us to dog number three. River explained that he was much younger than the other two and came from a bad shelter, so he could be skittish but he wouldn't bite. She introduced him as Bates and once she let him out of the crate, it was clear he was a mama's boy.

Bates barked at us, standing next to his mom with his tail wagging like crazy. River was playing with his ears and loving on him as she started to walk up the stairs. We had come in through the garage door, which brought us to her basement apartment, so the stairs were taking her to the main floor. "Y'all can sit down here," River explained. "I am letting the pups out and talking to my parents. I texted my dad on the way here. Their dogs are up so mine can go out quickly." We nodded our understanding as she walked away.

Raven was looking at River's book collection and I had a feeling I was going to be adding a lot more books to her collection as she grabbed her phone and started snapping pictures of books. I internally signed for our bank account, then it hit me that it would only take more of a hit with two book nerds. Fuuuuuck. Raven and I sat together on the small gray sofa and waited for River. We could hear voices carrying

CHAPTER 32

down to her living room and I was glad to hear laughter. I didn't know what they were talking about, but the vibes in this home seemed great. When River came back downstairs, it sounded like a stampede; the dogs fast and leaving River in their wake. Well, Bates wasn't down here yet, but I got the feeling he was waiting on River. When she finally joined us, with Bates, she had three bottles of water that she passed out for us. Her eyes wouldn't meet mine and I got the feeling she was stressed about her space and worrying we'd judge.

"Okay," River started, but immediately stopped, clearly unsure how to start or what to say. So, I decided to be blunt and break the ice and fucking awkwardness. "So, ladies, do you care to tell me what took place in that church and why you both came out looking like you might need time in a confessional booth?" The laughter that came from both of them made it clear it was a good ice breaker.

River quickly sported a blush and Raven rolled her eyes. "Zane, let's just say I can never eat a church wafer again without thinking about River here." I felt my eyebrows hit my hairline, but decided I'd wait for the story. If I had anything to do with it, it'd be a good time for the three of us, but now was the time to be serious.

"River, I love your space. It feels so much like you; it's comforting." River was blushing again and I wondered how deep I could make her blush. "Can we talk about everything? I want to be sure everyone is safe and on the same page. I think the three of us could be great together, but we need to understand one another. River, can you tell us more about you and we can tell you about us and how we ended up together?"

The light in River's eyes dimmed, but she nodded and started talking. We listened closely as she detailed lighter aspects of her life. Her struggles in school, how she ended up working with kids, her love for dogs, and her love for family. Once she got all the basics out of the way, she took a deep breath, readying herself to tell us about her marriage. She told us how they met through friends, at a young age, and dated for a while before moving in together. She talked about how they both struggled with depression and staying on meds. As she talked she hunched deeper into herself, moving on to talk about the first time he threatened suicide. River mentioned how this quickly became his way of controlling her.

My heart sank the longer she talked. He threatened the life of Bates. Took a knife to some of her favorite items. Threw her makeup in the front yard. Yelled and screamed in her face. He broke her, broke her down till she felt so alone and like she had no one to turn to. River had been made to believe if she ever left, his death and suicide would be on her hands. I couldn't even begin to imagine the trauma that would leave on someone. Eventually she came to how it all ended. How he had been screaming at her for days; had her in tears at work when he called and yelled at her for his oversleeping and berating her into believing it was all her fault. They had decided to try and spend a good day together, but instead it had ended with 911 being called and her being left with PTSD, and audible and visual flashbacks of screaming and blood.

My heart broke the more she talked. The way she was holding onto Bates makes it clear to me that she had truly thought she was going to lose him. These dogs clearly meant the world to her. Knowing someone she loves (because I am aware that love will never go away; the man she fell in love with will always have a place in her heart) had threatened things that bring her joy was astonishing to me. After her story, River talked about

CHAPTER 32

how she knew she always made excuses for him because of his mental health. It was truly heartbreaking to hear what she'd been through before she even turned 31.

After she stopped talking, not because her story was over but because she was holding back tears, I started to tell her about Raven and I. How we met in school and really liked each other and had even started dating. How awkward it was when our parents met at the divorce lawyer, while leaving their spouses, and started dating. How when they got serious, we had to tell them we had been dating since before they met. That they were understanding, but hopeful we'd stop seeing each other when they got married. River made a face of disgust here, obviously upset that our parents had been thinking about their happiness over ours. I made it clear that we never stopped seeing each other and defeated the odds of how many high school sweethearts break up. I told stories of us sneaking around together when we moved into the same house, and all the times we almost got caught.

I told River about the time I was literally caught with my head between Raven's legs by our dad, who looked at us and said "at least you believe in the clit and can find it," before shutting the door and walking away. Raven had been mid orgasm and was so embarrassed, she refused to eat dinner with us. River started cracking up and gave Raven a hug for the embarrassment she'd experienced. Us sitting together just felt so right; it felt like home with everyone's laughter coming together in the most beautiful way.

After a few hours of us talking and getting to know each other, River could no longer hide the pain on her face. With how easily she could hide her feelings, it was hard to remember that she was just in a bad car accident, but the cast and bruises helped us remember. I started to tell River we were going to leave her to rest, but she stopped me. "I could really use y'all's help for a moment." She took a deep breath before continuing. "I really struggle asking for help. I have been forced to do everything alone for so long, but I am working on it. Anyways, I'm rambling. With my arm in this cast and with my body sore, I need help showering. I don't wanna fall and harm myself or our fetus." I like that she included Raven in the "our fetus" comment; it made me feel all warm and fuzzy. River told us that before she showered, she was going to let the dogs out and take some meds. Before she could tell me to wait for her, I went with her. I wanted to be able to help her whenever possible and show her she was not alone.

Once upstairs, we let the dogs out and I looked around. When she said her parents were hippies, she wasn't joking; there's decor that shows a love for nature everywhere. While the dogs were in the backyard, I looked at the photos on the wall. I could easily tell by the smiles, which of the kids in the photos was River; it is such a beautiful smile. I was sad to see that some of the joy that was once in her eyes had definitely dimmed, and I had to wonder if her husband was the only one to put the blame for that on. I wanted to know everything. All her trauma. All her happy. All her wins. Everything.

I startled her when I said, "I hope our little one has your smile." The change in her expression had a frown coming to my face. That's when I heard footsteps behind me. Shit, she hadn't wanted to tell her parents yet. "River," her dad said, "how are you feeling?" She smiled warmly at him; the love and safety she felt, clear to see in her eyes. Seeing the love they shared eased something in my chest, knowing she has people

CHAPTER 32

that care about her here. "I'm feeling fine, Dad. This is Zane. He and Raven are helping me with a few things before they leave so I can rest tonight."

I moved forward, putting my hand out for him to shake. "Hey, I'm Zane. We met briefly at the hospital. I did River's tattoo and we really clicked. I realized that I desperately need to get to know this amazing woman more." He looked me up and down. "I'm Jake. Glad to see my girl getting back out there after all the bullshit with that ass she married." I blinked, stunned by the visceral anger in his voice. It was clear he holds anyone that hurts his daughter in low regard. Or is it daughters? I suddenly can't remember if River had siblings. So much to learn, so little time with our little one growing inside of her. After chatting a little more, I realized just how much I liked him. He was funny and full of love. Once he said he was going to bed, we said goodnight. That was when I realized that he was only in his underwear. This random man, that I don't know, just had a long conversation with me, and his daughter, in nothing but a white t-shirt. The boxer briefs were too small for comfort.

My eyes shot up and met River's, and the laughter in them let me know she was waiting for me to notice. Once Jake was gone she said, "That's my dad; a white man that fits a lot of the stereotypes. But he's a great dad." We got the dogs inside and started walking downstairs. Once we were in her private space I asked, "What stereotypes?" A surprised, joyful laugh escaped her and she said, "Ya know, lack of seasoning. Not necessarily the best at washing himself. Hell, I'm not even sure that he washes his hands after he pees." I stopped at that, because I just shook that man's hand. "River, where's your bathroom so I can wash my hands?" She laughed loudly as she pointed and I rushed to the bathroom.

After my hands were clean, River took her meds and got in the shower. I turned to Raven and with no explanation I said, "Flash me, please." She looked so confused, but did just that. I don't even think she realized she was going to do it. She flashed me and I stared at her beautiful tits and hard nipples, while I tried to get Jake's short, tight boxers out of my head. When she put her shirt down and unsurprisingly asked about my request, I told her. Now she was laughing so hard she could barely breathe and soon I was joining in.

After River finished her shower, Raven and I made sure she was comfortable and got her into bed. She asked for some water and kisses. We happily gave them to her and a beautiful smile took over her face. While our lips were locked, there was suddenly a dog tongue on my cheek; all three of her dogs clambered up to get between us. The laughter that broke out between the three of us was magical.

Once River was settled, Raven and I headed home. It really sucked that we had two separate cars because I really wanted to talk to her about what happened. I followed Raven home and groaned when I saw Dakota's car in the driveway. With everything that had happened, I really should not have been surprised; Raven would want to talk to them. We both got out of our cars and started walking up to the house. When we got to the door, Dakota was there with their eyebrow raised. "Care to explain? Raven, I was here hours ago for our friends night." Raven winced, probably feeling guilty for leaving Dakota waiting, despite knowing they wouldn't care. Hell, Dakota had a key to our home, so they were fine.

Chapter 33

Raven

I was so screwed. I knew I was gonna have to answer all of Zane's questions but now Dakota was here and they'd hear everything. Also, the shit they're gonna give me for showing up so late and forgetting our friends' night... fuck it'll be a long night. After we were all inside, sitting on the sofa with the cats and drinks, Zane just let the words out. "Raven, care to mention why I found you and River disheveled, smelling like sex, in your childhood home church?" His eyebrows were quirked and I watched in real time as Dakota's mouth dropped open, pretty comically. I could feel the blush and warmth hitting my cheeks; what a way to let Dakota know!

Since Zane decided to drop the news just like that, I wanted to make them both suffer. "I'll tell y'all shortly; I have to run upstairs and wash the communion juice off me." Before they could respond, I was up and running to the shower, leaving them to sit with their questions. I didn't rush my shower, enjoying the fact that they were having to sit in suspense, not knowing what had happened and why I was washing off juice. I was a little sad to wash off the memories, but the sensory overload of the stickiness was so uncomfortable. In hindsight, I should have hopped in the shower with River at her place, but oh well.

Once I finished showering, I hopped into some short PJ shorts that were covered in cats and an oversized black t-shirt, and headed back downstairs. Zane always went crazy when I wore these shorts and I loved torturing him. Look at me being all strategic. He was going to get to look at my legs and cusp of my ass while imagining River going down on me in a church, while I tell the story. The thought of teasing him and making him hard had me running my thighs together to get some friction. I loved being a tease; it always made me so wet.

Once I was back downstairs, I sat next to Zane and put my long dark legs out so they were on his lap. I could feel a bulge under my legs and it brought a smirk to my lips. I sighed, both due to the bulge and the comfort I got when he started stroking my legs. His thumb was moving back and forth over my leg; it's such a habit and so comforting. Before I could sink too far into his comfort and touch, Dakota said "speak".

I started by telling them how I stole River's contact from Zane's phone. Then I went on to tell them about how I asked her out and took her on a date. We laughed about how all she wanted was a waffle house, but all our hearts broke when I told them about how she struggled in Target. That led to me explaining why I brought her to the church for some peace and got us talking about our memories and how we shared them and opened up to each other and how amazing it was.

After I explained all the PG aspects of our date, I decided to go into great detail about how we were going to hell. I could see Zane working on controlling himself to not grab me and fuck me, as I talked about what River did with the communion juice and wafers. God, teasing and taunting him was so fucking hot. I loved when he went all caveman on me. Dakota could obviously

CHAPTER 33

see how close he was to taking me, because they said "Just go upstairs. I see that look in your eye Zane. I'll hang with the cats until you're done with my best friend."

Zane didn't need to be told twice. Next thing I knew, I was over his shoulder and there was a hard smack on my ass. I moaned loudly, forgetting my best friend was in the room with us, but Zane didn't because he growled, "save those sexy sounds for me. The rest you make tonight are all mine." I couldn't help but moan again at his words, earning me another smack and a loud groan from Dakota, causing me to laugh out loud.

Zane rushed us upstairs, yelling to Dakota that he planned on fucking me rough and fast. The laughter following us up the stairs told me Dakota wasn't sure about that. Dakota decided to taunt him further by yelling back, "I bet you can't keep it under 10 minutes!" Dakota knew that would taunt him into being as fast as possible.

When we got upstairs, Zane growled in my ear that he was gonna have me coming in 5 minutes and he'd be done in 7. I laughed, knowing it would just egg him on. Before I realized what was happening, my shorts were pulled to the side and his fingers were sliding through my wet heat, which just confirmed for him that I was ready for his cock. Before he thrust in, he reached over into the bedside table and grabbed the wand, turning it to my favorite setting. Zane pressed it down on my clit and I moaned loudly, forgetting once again that Dakota could hear me. Before I could worry about my noise level, he thrust in, hitting me as deeply as he could. I screamed, making it clear to everyone that I was in the bliss that comes with the pleasure he brings me.

He thrust in and out, deep and slow, hitting me deeply, keeping me moaning loudly. I guess it wasn't loud enough, because he held the wand on my clit, causing me to hit my climax, my pussy clenching around his cock. Once I became sensitive, I tried to push the wand away. Zane held it in place, growling that I owed him one more for being a whore of a tease. The dirty, degrading words had another loud moan leaving me. Zane kept up the punishing thrusts and the pressure from the wand. As pleasure took over my body again, I felt his hot cum filling my pussy.

Zane moved the wand away and pulled out of me. He ran to the door, which I was just now realizing was not shut all the way like I thought, and yelled down to Dakota that he won the bet. I knew I would be blushing hard when we got downstairs. Zane put the wand in the bathroom to be cleaned, grabbed me some panties, and when I gave him a confused look, he answered me saying "I want to know my cum is inside you and making your panties sticky while we talk to Dakota."

When we finally made it downstairs and were seated back on the couch, I noticed the shit eating grin on Zane's face and I was immediately worried, considering how much he liked to embarrass me.

Chapter 34

Zane
Knowing Raven was filling her panties with my cum had me getting hard all over again. I am so glad her legs were thrown over my lap because Dakota would be getting an eyeful in these gray sweatpants. I knew Raven saw the smirk on my face, but I planned on making her wonder about why I was smirking for a while. I took out my phone and shot River a text.

Zane: So, I hear you're hell bound for what happened in Raven's old church. Sleep well, beautiful.

River didn't respond and I could only hope that was because she had passed out and was resting. After how crazy hectic the last few days had been, she and our baby needed the rest. I could only imagine how emotionally draining the days had been for her. I must have zoned out, deep in thought about the last few days and River, because when I blinked both Raven and Dakota were staring at me. It was obvious I had missed something, so I decided to be obnoxious. I smirked and opened an app on my phone. I looked down at it and pressed a button. Suddenly, there was a gasp from Raven, who squeezed her legs shut, obviously trying to hide her reactions to the buzzing in her panties from Dakota. I honestly had no idea how she didn't realize the panties I put on her had a vibrator in them, but it felt like a win.

I don't acknowledge what I've done, excited for this game I started, and look at Dakota, asking them to repeat their question. We talked for a while, answering each other's questions. It was a great time, especially since I am having a blast tormenting Raven. She was squirming, enjoying the friction, fighting the embarrassment, and frustrated that as soon as she was close, I would change the settings. Edging Raven is one of my favorite past times; she won't be allowed to come until there were tears. Luckily, Dakota knew my plan, as I had texted them when we were still upstairs to be sure they were comfortable with this.

My hard on was trying to bust through my pants, but I wouldn't be getting any relief until Raven comes hard on this couch. Dakota had a smirk on their face that told me how much they enjoy watching their best friend squirm. I wanted to hear Raven go into even more details about her adventure in the church with River, because it would make her squirm even more. I started asking her more details, my mouth salivating at the thought of licking juice off Raven's body like River did. God, I wish I could have seen them together, but I am so glad they were bonding on their own. I wanted this to work and I needed them to like each other.

I decided to ramp up the vibration in her panties as she told us about River eating communion bread covered in her juices, and Raven moaned loudly, obviously forgetting that we had an audience! It brought me so much joy hearing her lose herself to pleasure and not worrying about the consequences of anyone seeing her. I felt like I was a teenager again, about to come in my pants at just the sounds of her pleasure.

Once she had finished riding the wave of her pleasure, I made sure to turn off her panties, and excused myself to the restroom. I think it was pretty obvious to everyone what I was about to do, but I truly did not care. Once I was in the privacy of our small half bath that Raven had decorated in light blues and grays, I propped my phone up on the counter and opened Snapchat. I set it to record and pulled my hard length from my sweats. I wanted Raven to know exactly what she does to me, and River too if she gave me permission to send her nudes. Luckily, we had body oil in all of our bathrooms, so I poured some in my hand and wrapped it around my length. I started to stroke myself, squeezing the base tightly; it didn't take me long to get close. I wanted to be sure I had a perfect cum shot, so I aimed directly at my phone and moaned loudly as I came, making sure I missed my phone but had a perfect splatter.

I saved the video to my camera roll, sent it to Raven, and got cleaned up before I headed back. Raven didn't have her phone out, so I could only assume she decided not to open it right now. I sat back down, and we chatted more and had a great time together. We always have such a great time together; it makes me so happy and so content. The only thing that could make it better was River and our baby. I could just imagine us all sitting here with a toddler that doesn't have an off button and causes all sorts of havoc. It just seemed so perfect.

After hours of talking and hanging out, Dakota decided it was time to go to bed, so Raven and I headed upstairs for some alone time. I didn't want to do anything sexual, but I wanted just the two of us to talk to see how she was feeling. I knew that her adventure in the church was fun, but also it was probably a taxing day. River was going through a lot and I could only imagine how hard it was to see her break enough to bring her somewhere Raven considered a sanctuary.

Once we were in the bed with the cats, after doing our night time routines, I held her tight and asked her about her mental health. Raven opened up about how hard it was to watch River break and how scary it was to hear her concerns. Raven told me how she still purchased the baby things for River, as a surprise, but she wouldn't give them to her till she was ready. We talked about River's fears surrounding her pregnancy and how we could help calm her nerves about the situation. We discussed moving our appointments for all the OB/GYN appointments, that way we could be there every step of the way and show River that she wasn't alone. We decided we needed to take her out together and separate, and woo her in every way possible. We wanted her to feel as special as possible, and show her how she should have been treated this entire time.

Chapter 35

Zane

It had been a few weeks since I caught my girls in the church, still one of my favorite spank bank items, and Raven and I had made sure to spoil River in every way possible. Today was a big and busy day. River had several doctors appointments today. She was getting checked out after her accident, her cast off, and her first baby appointment! Raven and I made sure to take off for today; we wanted to be there to be supportive and see/hear our baby. I have on black sweats and a t-shirt from the shop. Raven steps out of the bathroom with a light face of makeup, hot pink leggings (that I love watching her ass in) and a bookish shirt that says "give me all the villains." I hold back a snort laugh. She might like to read about villains, but in reality she wants a caring man who will treat her like she's a slut when we're in bed.

Once we're ready, we go to pick up River to get breakfast before our long day. As we pull up to pick up River, I roll down the window and whistle; she looks adorable. A short pink dress, with quarter length sleeves, and black biker shorts peeking underneath. Once we're all in the car, we head to a local breakfast shop. Once we're seated at a booth, the two girls on one side and me on the other, we start looking at the menu, and

I can hear River making noises. I honestly can't tell if they're good or bad sounds, but she suddenly stands up and rushes to the restroom. Raven gets up and follows her, asking me to order River a water and sprite and an OJ and water for herself.

I honestly don't know what to think of everything that just happened. I'm so very shocked, I don't even know what to think. The waiter comes over and I order 3 waters, two OJ's, and a Sprite with no ice. Even though River isn't at the table I do remember her saying she does not like ice in her soda; it waters them down or something. The girls are gone for a few minutes and when they finally return, River looks a little green and worse for wear. When they're both seated again, I look at River and ask if she's okay. "Yeah, my morning sickness has been ramping up the last few days."

"Why didn't you tell me, we could have brought you Pepto," I say. "Zane, it is really okay. I knew we were going to the doctor today, and they would give me meds. There is a long list of shit I can't have and I do not want to risk anything. I have had so many health issues, and don't want to risk this. It's all I've ever wanted and my late husband made sure I would not ever have a kid with him. We thought I couldn't get pregnant, ya know the endometriosis and PCOS, so we tried to foster and eventually adopt. They asked him to see a mental health professional and he refused to see someone. It was to make sure the kids would be safe. So, I plan on being the best possible pregnant person." I smile, knowing I plan on making sure I am there for everything and supporting her in every way possible. Even if we don't work out, even though I think we will, I will be there for her in every single way possible. She and our kid will know the best love and support I can provide.

Our waiter comes back before I can respond and takes our

CHAPTER 35

orders. River orders french toast, Raven orders pancakes with eggs and sausage, and I order an omelet with a side of pancakes. "River," I say, "I want you to know I will be there for you and our child no matter what. I know Raven will be too." I see Raven smile and nod in confirmation. "So please ask us for any support you need." I can see River starting to tear up, so I decided to change the subject.

"Are you sure you just want french toast? There's no protein in that." She gives me a sad smile. "A lot of people judge me for eating more, because I'm fat. But that doesn't usually hold me back. Today it's because I don't think my stomach can handle more." She must see me get ready to argue over her "fat" comment, because she shakes her head and smiles. "I don't mean fat in a bad way; society has made it a bad word but it's just my body. I am fat and I've learned to like and accept my body. I'm not unhealthy and my fat is a symptom of other things. Yes, I struggle and sometimes limit what I eat because of it. So, I appreciate you caring and not judging. My late husband used to judge me a lot and say things he knew would hurt me."

"It will definitely be an adjustment to not think of fat as a bad or insulting word. But I will do anything for you and will never judge you. You're stunning just the way you are."

After our food comes, which I notice makes River look a little green, I decide to change the topic. I want to talk about our baby and parents. "Okay, I have some serious questions. "When do you think we should tell our parents?" I swear River turns even more green, but she swallows her food and bites her lip. I can tell biting her lip is something she does when she's thinking. "Well, a fetus is considered viable at 24 weeks, but I think that's a long time to carry this secret. Besides, my parents have been noticing I don't feel well. It's been pretty obvious that I can't hold down food, but I think right now they're blaming trauma. Eventually they'll ask questions, especially since y'all have been around."

"So, after the appointments, when we leave with images, let's get on Etsy and order them presents to announce it. They can be made with each grandparent in mind! That also gives us the time of them being made as a safety net and introducing the others as partners? If y'all are okay with being my partners?" I swear my heart grows two sizes hearing she wants to introduce us, and be introduced as partners. "River, I absolutely want that. I know that is what Raven wants too. How will your parents react to a queer poly relationship? Correct me if I'm wrong, but you have only ever been in cis relationships?"

River takes another bite of french toast before shocking me with her answer. "A few months before my late husband died, I came out to my mom as bi. It was part of me working up to getting ready to admit I was gonna ask for a divorce. Not too long ago I told her I would no longer do monogamous relationships and I am more interested in Poly. I also told them I would never get married again. So, I definitely don't think they'll be shocked to be honest." The smile that took over my face was big and bright. "What? Why are you smiling like that, Zane?" she asks. "Because you are so strong and I am so, so proud of you princess. It could not have been easy to tell them all of that, especially given everything y'all have been going through."

"I mean, I was definitely worried. They're both white people who are 60. But my younger sibling paved the way. They don't go by norms, and my best friend, Fe, is trans and poly. So, none of this is new to them. But I do think it was a slight shock, given I have only been in cis het monogamous relationships. Either

CHAPTER 35

way, they'll be supportive even if they don't understand. But, I have had something on my mind and I want to run it by y'all."

Before I can respond, Raven does, telling River we're here to listen and how excited she is for our futures. River then goes on to tell us how she knows that gender reveal parties are all the rage but she thinks they only reinforce gender norms. She doesn't want one and she thinks we should do everything gender neutral, including the name. That way our child can learn who they are on their own; the only people who need to know will be those who have to change their diaper. It's clear to me that she was worried about bringing this up to us, because she continues before we can reply. She tells us she used to always plan on naming her kids after family members, but they aren't considered gender neutral and she wants our child to feel as loved and accepted as possible.

I'm not sure how to respond; it's clear she's put a ton of thought into this and how to make sure our child feels as loved and respected as possible. Raven saves me from coming up with words that I am sure will be inadequate in describing how much her thoughts warm my heart. Raven's voice cracks as she tells River how much her love for our unborn child is showing and how heartwarming it is to know the support they're already getting inside the womb.

We move to less heavy topics as we finish breakfast and just get to know each other more. It already feels so much like a family and I love it. We finish eating, pay, and head to the car. Our first doctor's appointment of the day is a check up for River following her wreck. We wait for what feels like hours before they call her back. River goes back alone, while Raven and I wait in the waiting area. It doesn't take too long before River comes out looking upset, but says she's been given a clean bill of health from the wreck. Her cast is scheduled to come off in another few weeks, but everything else seems to be healing well. When I finally get a chance to ask her what's wrong, she tells us the nurse made a comment about her weight. It's clear it hurt her, but it's also something she tells us she faces all the time.

Her OB/GYN is in the same doctors office complex; is that what it's called? So, we sit down at a local coffee shop next door, and get on Etsy ahead of time. River tells us she wants to get her dad a Falcons baby announcement and her mom like a blanket. River decides her dad would love a coffee mug, and maybe a matching one for my mom since they're married. Her mom loves anything floral, so she's thinking of a framed ultrasound in a floral border. My dad is the hardest, so I decided to go simple. He likes totes to go shopping, so a canvas tote with the ultrasound that says "grandpa to be." We keep searching for the best shops on Etsy, having so much fun that we almost ignore the timer for the OB/GYN. However, the draw of seeing our little one wins out.

Luckily, when River scheduled the appointment she told them all three of us are going into the room. She did request for us to go straight to the room and not to see her weight. It's clear that this is something she really struggles with, but I want her to know we think she is beautiful and her weight is a part of that. The number on a scale does not determine anyone's worth; there is so much more to people than their weight.

Once we get into her doctor's office, she walks up and checks us in, reminding them we're all going back. Luckily, the doctor's office now has all the paperwork filled out online prior to appointments, so once she got checked in, we sat in the waiting room and waited. River was playing with her

CHAPTER 35

hair and I saw a knot forming. I remember her mentioning her Trichotillomania in a text, so I reached over and grabbed her hand letting her know she's not alone. She smiled at me gratefully before grabbing her hair back and putting her hair in a messy bun. I hated that this situation was stressing her out so much, but she also shared with me that she struggled with Trichotillomania her entire life. It's a compulsion she cannot control and it gets worse with stress. We sat in the waiting room holding hands, until they finally called her back.

River asked what room we're gonna be in so Raven and I can head that way while they take her weight. Once they said 8, Raven and I headed that way and I heard River take a deep breath to prepare for having her weight taken. I hate how much society puts on a person's size; it's such bullshit. Once Raven and I are in the room I grab her, hug her tight and plant a big, wet kiss to her lips. I could not ask for a better partner to go through all of this with, and I told her as much. We sit in the chairs and wait for River; I swear we're squeezing hands so tight they are near breaking.

River comes in and the nurse instructs her to strip and put on the gown and she'll be back in a few. River does as asked, and I can see her hands shaking from here, but I don't bring it up because adding to her stress would be a dick move. Raven, however, stands up, walks over to River, gives her a huge hug and whispers in her ear. The comfort they bring each other warms my heart. I am so lucky they're in my life. Raven helps get River situated and moves her chair over so she's sitting next to her and can hold her hand. There is a slight knock on the door and the doctor asks to come in. River responds in a small voice, but it's clear the doctor hears her and enters. When she sees my girls sitting next to each other, a smile takes over her face and she tells River she's glad she has support.

When she asks River what's going on, there is clear shock on her face. Especially when she hears about how River learned she was pregnant and how unprofessional her late husband's dad acted. She asks some basic questions, like does she know who the father is. River nods and introduces me. When she asks River how far along she is, River is able to give her the exact date of her tattoo. The date puts her at about 3 months along; it's weird to think that about 6 months from now, we'll have a baby. She's due January 1st, we'll literally be starting 2025 with a new dynamic.

The appointment goes by quickly and the doctor gives River some more basics about the pregnancy. They do classify her as a "high risk" pregnancy because of her weight and PCOS. We're told it's a good idea to buy a blood pressure cuff to make sure it stays at a healthy level. With some more basic information given, the doctor tells us she is done and the ultrasound technician will be in shortly.

Raven is holding River's hand tightly and I can see the stress in River's eyes. Her left hand keeps going to her hair, and it's like she catches herself and brings it back down. When she catches me watching her, she looks down; the shame she feels over her compulsion is clear. I can't stand seeing her ashamed over something she can't control, so I stand, walk over to her, grab her chin and make her look me in the eyes. I'm not anticipating a response to my actions, but she talks before I can. "*He*", it's clear who he is, "used to yell at me every time my hands were near my hair. I truly think he thought he was helping, but honestly it always made it worse. I literally cannot control it. Does anyone really think I want a random section of my hair to be shorter than the rest? I was always so

CHAPTER 35

embarrassed and full of shame whenever he did it."

There is really nothing I can say to help, so I lean down and press a kiss to her lips. The door opens right then and the ultrasound tech walks in. "Oh, excuse me," she murmurs in a quiet voice, "should I give y'all a minute?" We all quickly assure her she's fine; it's pretty clear we're all ready to see our little one. The tech gets everything ready and tells us what is going to happen. She says the baby won't be too big and placement plays a big role and how good the image will be. I decided against going back to my chair, instead deciding to stand by the other side of River. She's too low down to wrap my arms around, but I grab her hand and hold it to my chest. I am sure she can feel my heart beating at a crazy fucking rate.

The tech warns River that the gel would be cold before squeezing it all over her belly. You can't tell if she's growing yet, but I doubt it'll be much longer now! The tech takes a few minutes finding the baby and suddenly the room is filled with a "thud, thud, thud" and the screen shows a tiny little thing. The ultrasound tech tells us everything looks great, measuring at 1.5 inches. It's surreal, my life changed so much with one tattoo, and I am so grateful it did. After moving the wand around some more for different images, she prints them out, cleans off River's belly, and tells her to get dressed and the doctor will be right back. On her way out though she hands me a box of tissue, and it's then that I realize I'm crying. They're the happiest of tears.

Chapter 36

River

At the end of my appointment, I scheduled a follow up for about 2 months out and we headed to the car. My stomach was a disaster, ready to absolutely blow. It felt like waves were rocking a boat that was much too small for the natural disaster that was hitting it. Which honestly felt like an accurate description of my life in general; a boat too heavy for its small frame being put against the torment that is life. I know my therapist wants me to work on not thinking like that, but it is so hard. Maybe things are starting to brighten up. Zane, Raven, and our little one are all signs of a brighter horizon.

Once we're in the car, Zane asks if I'm hungry. The people pleaser side of me wants to tell them that if they want food, I'll sit with them, but I really just want to go home and rest. So, I do something that is uncharacteristic of me and speak up. "I actually would just love a Sprite and to go home. We can pull out my laptop, get on Etsy, order gifts, and just relax. My stomach's a mess and I want it to calm down before I formally introduce y'all to my parents." I don't express my fears that I am running out of time to be honest about who they are to me. My parents aren't stupid. They may not be as up to date, but they're better than most; I mean, I might be biased, but I think they're better.

CHAPTER 36

Zane agrees and starts to head in the direction of my home. He stops at a drive-through, gets food for him and Raven, and a Sprite for me. When we get to the house, Zane helps me let the dogs out while Raven takes all the food and drinks into the basement. My mutts are always ecstatic to see them, and it makes it feel so much more right. They're my babies and they have to approve. Luckily, my parents aren't home, so we get the dogs out and back in without interruption. Once we were back downstairs, I lay my head on Zane's lap on the couch. Raven's in my oversized leather chair with dogs surrounding her, begging for food; they were quick to learn that Raven's a sucker for their puppy dog eyes.

As they eat, I joke that Zane better not drop any food on my head. But life must have a sick sense of humor because his hamburger immediately spills ketchup and mustard under my nose, and my stomach rolls. I jump up, Zane and Raven cracking up, but they immediately stop as I rush to the bathroom. I shut the door and barely make it to my knees in time before my stomach is emptying. I hear pounding footsteps and someone comes up behind me, holding my hair back so it doesn't get dirty. When I get a chance to breathe, I smell Zane's rich earthy scent and try to send him away. He should be eating, not worrying about me. But instead, he wets a washcloth and wipes the condiments off my face, kissing my forehead. As sweet as it is, my stomach rolls again and I'm turned back to the porcelain throne, giving it an offering no one wants to see.

It's not long before a cool washcloth is placed on the back of my neck. When it touches my skin, I become aware of just how much Zane has been doing to take care of me. He's been whispering sweet nothings in my ear and making sure I'm comfortable while my stomach throws temper tantrums. The thought of just how much he's been doing for me, has me blinking back tears. It's not long before the tears start to stream down my face, and then wracking sobs race through my body. I wish I could kiss him, but seeing as how the taste in my mouth has me gagging, I won't do that to this wonderful man.

Once my stomach has decided that it's done trying to expel itself, I stand up with Zane's help, and wash my mouth out. Unfortunately, every time I am sick like this, my migraines kick up a notch. I'm usually good at ignoring them, but now I can't. I honestly do not know how I am supposed to function when I go back to work on Monday. Luckily, I have a few days to rest but I also have to disclose my pregnancy. That's something to worry about another day.

When we leave the bathroom, Raven has a weird look on her face. At first I'm worried that she's upset that Zane ran to my aid. As I'm trying to bring it up (ya know, being new to poly and everything means navigating new experiences), I see a certain dog with red on its snout. I start laughing because it's clear the dogs took full advantage of Zane and Raven being cat people and stole his food the minute he got up. I immediately start laughing harder, because welcome to my life, bitches.

I can't take my migraine meds because of my pregnancy, so I get a big cup of water and head to lay down in the dark. Raven follows me, while Zane sulks about his food, and she asks me what's wrong. I explain to her how the constant exorcism of my stomach causes my migraines to get exponentially worse. All I wanted to do is lay down in the dark. Raven, the amazing woman she is, sits down on my bed and lets me lay my head in her lap while she plays with my hair. Having my hair played with is one of the most relaxing things in this world. It always has me feeling content and cared for, and that's all I need right

CHAPTER 36

now.

While we lay in the dark, she pulls her phone out, putting the eye comfort shield on and turning the brightness down, to help my head, and gets on Etsy. We spend the next hour adding items to the cart and deciding what to get for all our parents. It is frustrating because I just want everyone to love their gift and feel involved. Eventually everything was ordered and we asked them for shipping around two weeks. To prevent my parents from accidentally opening theirs early, all the gifts were sent to Raven's and Zane's house. It is such a relief to have them ordered and makes everything feel so real. How has this become my life? It's not long after that the exhaustion, pain, and hair stroking has me falling asleep with my head in Raven's lap.

Chapter 37

Raven

Sitting in River's bed, her head in my lap, listening to her soft snores filling the room, feels so right. I know her life, chronic illness, and now pregnancy has been hard on her, so bringing her this comfort makes my chest flutter. Zane walks in, followed by 3 big dogs, with a scowl on his face. I'll admit I saw the dogs going for his food, but honestly did not think they'd actually grab it. They're River's babies, they deserve treats.

"I am gonna get River's phone, call her dad, and let her dogs out. You keep cuddling her; I don't want them to wake her to go out and her dad's met me before. I'm sure he'll have several questions, but we'll deal with it as a team when she's awake." I nod my head, not wanting to disturb River.

My fingers keep running through her hair and a small frown takes over my face when my fingers get caught on a large knot. I take my time untangling it, trying not to hurt River. Once I get that one out, I find another small one and get to work on it. It's heartbreaking to see the evidence of her stress and compulsion. I want to be sure she feels supported and cared for. While I know her parents are amazing at that, it's clear that her past partners have not been. Zane and I are on the same page about changing

CHAPTER 37

that. We're going to show her everything she deserves and has never had, and there is no doubt in our minds she'll do the same for us.

Zane comes back and the dogs' thundering steps follow him. Once they're in the bedroom, all three dogs jump on the bed and cuddle as close as they can to River. They cover her in soft licks; I get the feeling they're worried for her and want to make sure she's okay. The love of a pet is truly one of unwavering care and support. Once everyone is settled, Zane gets River's phone plugged in and puts on a book. This shocked me and I gave him a questioning look. He whispered to me, "once, she told me she needs the sound of a comfort book to sleep. So she has several she can play to fall asleep; I just put on one she mentioned in the past. Zodiac Academy is one of her favorites, so I took an educated guess." I nod that I understand. Really not wanting to disturb River, we both kissed her forehead and headed to the car.

It's been a few weeks since River's doctor's appointment and now it's time to meet her family. She did tell us she told them about us and they're so excited to meet us. They're thrown by the idea of a poly relationship, but they truly just want their daughter safe and happy. We met them at a local Italian restaurant. River picked it because it has light options that are less likely to upset her stomach. I have on a dark pair of skinny jeans and a turquoise crop top with flowers on it. Zane looks amazing in light jeans and a black button up with his sleeves rolled up, showing off his forearms and the amazing tattoos covering his body. When we planned this dinner, we decided to wait on the pregnancy announcement. If everything goes well, we will have all the grandparents over for a meal to eat, meet, and open presents.

The meal is amazing. River has an oversized green t-shirt that says "dog mom" and black leggings. It's pretty clear to me and Zane that she's trying to hide her belly, which gets harder every day for her. She's recovered fully from her car accident and is doing really well. Both her parents sing our praise for taking care of their "baby girl" and doing everything we can to help her recover. They are extremely open, honest, and accepting. I won't lie and say I wasn't worried, our relationship is unconventional, but they have no problem with it. When River excused herself to the restroom, her mom looked at us and said, "I don't give a fuck about y'alls relationship. I won't judge. As long as you treat our girl right, we'll support you. But she has been through hell already; don't do what that douche bag she married did. I didn't learn about the abuse till after his suicide, which in itself was a form of abuse, and I want her to have the relationship, or is it relationships because it's poly, she deserves." Dinner goes by quickly and Zane pays the check before her parents can try to. River has a smile on her face that won't quit, and when our eyes met she nodded, giving me permission to ask. I tell them about the family meal and ask them to join. They agree and it's on. We have a week to prepare and tell everyone of the change. River wanted Fe and Dakota there too, for mental support. It is going to be a wonderful evening.

The next week was full of shopping, cleaning, and preparing. We're all still busy with work, but luckily the shop is closed on Sundays so we didn't have to reschedule anything for dinner. After all, we've got a baby to support. We need to work as much as possible. River came over for dinner two days ago,

CHAPTER 37

we wrapped all the presents and went over the menu. Zane is cooking hot dogs on the grill, fruit, and some chips. Laid back for all involved.

When the day comes River and her parents get there immediately after our parents. Dakota and Fe have been here for hours setting up with us, and I might have seen some flirting there. Everyone seems to be getting along amazingly. River's dad seems to be the king of dad jokes, with some that she's really embarrassed by. Once everyone has been introduced, we start talking. Zane's grilling and it is one of the best days. It feels like a family and everything feels so right. We're all sitting around on the back porch, eating, laughing, and having a great time.

We spent several hours eating and laughing, it was wonderful. Once it seemed like everyone was finished eating, I asked River to help me bring the dishes inside. Her doctor had called in some pregnancy safe nausea meds, so she was actually able to eat today. Once inside, I planted a big kiss on her lips, telling her how wonderful today is going and how I am so thankful she's in our lives. The smile on her face and the way she kisses me back tells me she feels the same. When I ask if she's ready to share the presents, her hands immediately go into her hair, telling me how stressed she is about this. She had shared her concerns about our parents not knowing her and not approving, and Zane and I had done everything in our power to assure her everything would be amazing.

The presents are hidden in our pantry, because who would go in there, and we grab them and walk outside. The grandparent-to-be look at us with obvious confusion as to why we have presents, but don't ask questions, which seems a little strange to me. I make sure they all know not to open their gifts until I say so, that way they all find out about the same time. When I hand

River a gift, she looks at me with even more confusion than our parents, because obviously she knows she's pregnant. "Ready, set, open!" I yell and everyone but River starts opening their presents. I knew she wouldn't open hers till all the parents had and that's what we wanted. Zane and I wanted her to experience the joy of our parents presents before the joy of hers.

Slowly, all the parents get their presents open and can't keep the confused looks off their faces. They start looking at everyone's presents, as if to clarify that what they're seeing is accurate. Suddenly, River's mom stands up, walks over to her, and gives her the biggest hug. She whispers something in River's ear, too quietly for me to hear, but they both have big smiles on their faces and tears streaming down. Zane walks up and gives them a big group hug. It's clear they're all so happy and I am loving soaking in all their joy. My parents walk up to me, confirming that I'm not upset with the situation. I say everything in my power to assure them I am stoked; full of life, and joy. I cannot express just how right it feels because it feels like something out of a romance book. Once our parents have calmed down, River opens her gift from Zane and I, and the tears and smiles come back in full force. It's a beautiful silver necklace with a heart pendant. In the heart are our three birthstones and we plan on adding the little one's birthstone as soon as they're here. We're here for the long haul.

Chapter 38

River

The party where we announced our pregnancy went so well. I could not be more excited and thankful for everyone in my life. Fe and Dakota were there as amazing moral support, all of the grandparents were ecstatic, and Raven and Zane were so supportive. I honestly can't believe this is my life, coming from my past relationships and the circumstances surrounding it. The other shocker for me was the support of their parents. My late husband's parents never liked or supported me, or us really, so I don't know how to react to all this support.

I had a virtual therapy session the day after the announcement and I could not control my joy. She was absolutely shocked and overjoyed. She made sure to tell me not to self sabotage. She wanted to be sure I knew it's not my job to decide if I'm too much for them; they're adults and can determine that. That's going to be my biggest hurdle, I really struggle with it. I have a habit of deeming myself unworthy and always putting myself down. While I know I have a lot of strengths, I'm kind, determined, loving, and supportive to name some, I tend to leave myself in the "traumatized fat widow" box which really does more harm than good but it's hard to overcome.

Today's a big day, Raven is meeting me at my OB/GYN appointment. Zane had to work but Raven's appointments were done for the day so she's here to support me. We're at my second ultrasound, now at the five month mark. It's going by so quickly. According to the app on my phone, my little bubble should be about a pound and the size of a bell pepper.

I won't lie, I am a little nervous without Zane, not because Raven isn't amazing, but because my ex's dad works in this medical building. I really do not want to run into that man again. He has a habit of knowing exactly what to say to break me and send me over the edge. Luckily, we didn't run into him on the way into the appointment and I am able to let out a relieved breath. I was truly worried he would ruin this appointment for me. When I walk into the waiting room, I see Raven sitting there waiting for me. I walk over to her and kiss her, claiming her as mine in front of the entire office, before walking to get checked in.

Everything went amazing during the appointment. We got to hear our little bubble and see them again. My blood pressure, heart rate, and vitals all look good. They did take some blood to make sure everything is fine, which brings a sense of comfort to me that they'll catch something if it's wrong. They ask if we want to know the sex of the baby and I am taken back. We don't care about the sex, everything we're doing is gender neutral, but Zane is not here and it feels wrong finding out without him. So, they write it down and put it in an envelope for us all to open together. Both bubble and I are given a clean bill of health and we schedule the next appointment. Raven's in the bathroom and I'm headed to my car when there's a shout behind me.

I've been embracing the pregnancy and have on a shirt that says "mama to be" and highlights my ever growing bump. As

CHAPTER 38

soon as I see him, I regret turning around. There he is, the man who hates me and blames me for his son's suicide. While I know it's not my fault, he has a way of convincing me it is. "Does the father of your bastard know you drove your partner to suicide? Is he aware that it will probably be his fate for sleeping with the slut you are?" The tears are immediately everywhere and people are stopping and watching. I manage to ask him to leave me alone, but my voice is weak and he ignores me.

"You don't deserve anything good in your life; you took my son from me. If he was going to end his life, he should have taken you with him. I would find comfort knowing your parents are suffering too and there would be justice, because it's all your fucking fault." He's screaming in my face, spit flying and hitting me, and other people aren't helping; they're just recording my pain. They don't care that he just said his son should have killed me? They don't care that he's harassing a pregnant woman, they're just letting it happen.

Suddenly, Raven is by my side. She's guiding me back into the office and tells me to sit and wait. I did as she asked; all the joy from today has left my body. Raven quickly left the office. I didn't know what she was doing, but she wasn't gone long. She then says something to the receptionist before kneeling on the floor in front of me. Raven gently wipes away my tears and kisses me all over. She doesn't ask me to talk, just waits with me. The receptionist calls her over, she whispers she'll be right back, and she walks over to talk to her. When Raven comes back, there is a cop with her. Fuck, I hate cops. She shows the cop something on her phone. I can hear the entire altercation playing over her speaker. It causes a shuddering breath to leave me; I don't want to have to listen to his hate again.

Raven informs the cops that she was in the bathroom when

the altercation started and got the recording from a bystander who just watched and recorded. The cops ask me some questions; I answer them all and tell him that this has happened before. He verbally attacked me in the hospital after my wreck, when I learned I was pregnant. I gave them all the details I could of both events. Unfortunately, my memory of the hospital is a little hazy, but I'm determined. I am not going to let this evil man ruin anything more for me. He is not going to get in the way of a happy relationship by using all the emotional abuse his son put me through.

Once we are finished speaking with the cop, they head down to his office and arrest him. I am pressing chargers; it will keep happening if I don't. Once it's safe, and the officer has him, we walk into his office and speak with the owner of the practice. I know I would not want someone like that attached to my practice. We tell him everything, and he assures us he will be removed from the practice. He even tells us he'll provide us with his lawyer and help us get a restraining order.

I'm a little shocked because I figured he'd be loyal to his coworker. I work up the courage to ask why he's helping me. His answer has my emotions going haywire again. Apparently he never liked the way he talked about me, and it only got worse after the suicide. He tried telling him that I was probably the main reason his son made it to 30, but he didn't want to hear it. He admits he wanted to get him help, but never wanted to overstep. So, now he's doing right by me. My late husband was like a son to him, and he knows I brought him joy and comfort. This is what he would want done in this situation. The reminder of the man my late husband used to be is both sad and happy. It wasn't all bad, it just ended in one of the worst ways possible.

CHAPTER 38

Raven and I thank him and decide we will take him up on his offer. Lawyers are expensive and there is only a small chance he will stay locked up. I know how the system works; he'll post bail and get something like community service. He's a wealthy white man, he won't do time. I just want him away from me and in therapy. I don't think prison would solve anything.

Raven and I leave the medical complex and have some girl time. I followed her to a local mall. Luckily my insurance gave me enough to get a decent used CR-V that I love, so I am able to drive again. We get to the mall and go straight to the food court, because I am starving. We went to the Chinese restaurant in the food court and ordered. I am so excited, greasy Chinese food is just what I need after the altercation. Once we binge on comfort food, we walk around the mall and shop.

We got baby goods, clothes, bottles, blankets, and more. I also got some more maternity clothes, because I'm obviously growing. It was a great time, and just what I needed. Raven and I came up with an amazing idea for how to pick our bubble's name. We even picked several names out to run by Zane. It is getting so close and *so* real. I cannot even express all the feelings that are taking over my body.

Chapter 39

Zane

I told Raven and River that I would be working late, but in reality my only appointment was early and I finished hours ago. I am now hard at work on a surprise for them; I'm not working alone, Fe and Dakota are here too. When Fe and Dakota aren't flirting, they're helping paint the walls of the nursery. Dakota is painting the top half of the walls sky blue, while Fe is painting the bottom half a forest green.

While painting the walls, I am painting clouds on the ceiling and applying those cute glow in the dark stars. As we work, we're deciding what to draw on each wall. I mean, I am an artist so I will be drawing all over the wall. One wall will have portraits of River's dogs, one will have Raven's and my cats, and then I will scatter wild animals throughout the other walls. Each wall will have trees and plants. I really want to make it feel like they're connected with nature. But the walls have to dry first, so once the base paint is done we get to working on some other important things.

River hasn't officially moved in yet, but we talked about it and she does plan to. This way, we're all together, can split responsibilities, and our relationship can continue to grow. It just feels so right. Being separate from River doesn't sit well

CHAPTER 39

with Raven and I; she's meant to be here. We haven't said the L word yet, but it is certainly coming, there is no doubt in my mind. Because we talked about her moving in, we decided to go ahead and order furniture for the nursery, and it was all delivered yesterday! Now that I am done with the ceiling and Fe and Dakota are almost finished with the walls, it's time to assemble the Ikea furniture. The three of us working together are able to assemble the furniture, with ample amounts of cussing, but it is so exciting to see all this work being done.

Once the furniture was successfully put together, I went back into the room to start painting the nature and animal scenes on the walls. It felt amazing to do art that will bring joy to my future. If I had known the art I did on River would change the trajectory of my family and joy forever, I would do nothing different. I do sometimes worry she'll run, or think she's too much, but we're working through that as a family.

The next few hours pass with me zoning into my painting and ignoring the rest of the room. Fe and Dakota are putting together the smaller items for the baby's room, like the mobile, and they're just leaving me to work. After hours of painting, I am finally on the last wall; it's been a process. Luckily, none of the walls started empty. One has a folding closet door, one has the bedroom door, another has a small bathroom door, and the last has windows. So, I was able to accomplish it in a day instead of several.

Once I am done painting, I go on the hunt for the two extras to see how they're coming along. They're sitting in the living room, flirting, watching documentaries, and slowly putting the items together. The living room is a disaster, there are boxes and protective packaging everywhere. The cats are obviously enjoying it though; they're jumping from one box to the next and running over the packaging like their lives depend on it. Maybe they do, I don't speak cat.

As soon as I get to cleaning up, my phone rings. It's like Raven is able to sense when my hands are full. Luckily Dakota is able to reach in my pocket and answer the phone on speaker. Apparently the two girls went shopping for baby stuff and headed home with it and pizza. Raven tells me their ETA and I cuss under my breath. The room is not dry enough to put all the furniture in, so they're not going to see it put together like I planned. But I do have enough time to clean, so I do. I get all the trash and recycling dealt with so the women don't walk into a mess. There is still some clutter on the floor from finishing assembling different items for the room, but it's a hell of a lot better.

When they get home, they're definitely taken back by the chaos in the living room. They obviously did not anticipate seeing the three of us hard at work getting things ready for everyone. River carried the pizza inside and Raven had multiple bags of baby things in her hands. I want to groan, because how much did that cost, but they could say the same thing about everything I have going on here. Soooo, oh well.

River immediately sat the pizza on the coffee table and plopped down. Raven sat the bags down and sat down next to River. I can tell something is wrong, but as I go to ask, Raven shot me a look. "River is hungry and thirsty, let's eat and we'll tell you about the day we had." Before I can go get drinks, Fe and Dakota are up and headed to the kitchen. They come back with five glasses of water, one with no ice for River, and five plates. Once we're all sitting with food and drinks, River tells us the doctor's appointment went well. She shows us the ultrasound images and tells us everything they checked. Then she takes a

CHAPTER 39

deep breath before telling us about her run in with her ex father-in-law. All the steps they took, the help his former coworker offered, and about how they went shopping to keep her mind off it.

She goes on to say how glad she is for her therapist, because if that had happened before her appointment, she's worried she would have pulled away. Her thoughts immediately following the altercation all circled around how she's too much for us. That she never intended to bring unnecessary drama to our lives and how she thought we might be better off without her. My emotions rush through me like a hurricane; worry over what could have happened if he got violent, relief that they're all three safe, and sadness that River has been made to think so little of herself. We all talk about what we need to do about him, because he doesn't deserve any real recognition. He is the lowest of low. We came to the conclusion that we will work with the lawyer to get a restraining order, because the cops will back him.

After we finished eating Raven and River showed us all of the baby stuff they got. Everything from a bunch of gender neutral clothes, to toys, pacifiers, bottles, a blanket, and socks. So many baby socks. After they showed me everything they got, I decided it was time to show them the nursery. I ask Dakota and Fe to cover the girls' eyes and lead them down the hall. This way they couldn't sneak a peak and they were not bumping into the furniture in the hallway.

"Okay," I said, "one, two, three.. Look". The audible gasps that leave them don't really tell me much, but I can assume that they like it. "Zane," River starts breathlessly, "this is amazing. You painted our fur babies on here and it is so beautiful. I can't believe you did all of this." She leans in and kisses me, hard.

Once she pulls away Raven is there kissing me, telling me how talented I am between kisses. Everyday I am reminded as to why I am the luckiest man in the world.

We all talk about the best places for the furniture and work out little details. That's when Fe and Dakota surprised the hell out of all of us; apparently they're planning a baby shower and wanted to pick a date with us. Since River is about 6 months along, they want to do it in about a month. That gives us a month to finish the room, make a registry, and move River in here. It will be a lot, but well worth it.

Raven then tells us that she and River have a special event that they want to happen at the baby shower. When they talk about the plan they came up with, smiles take over all of our faces. Dakota and Fe decide to leave; they both work early tomorrow and they did a lot of work here today.

Once they're gone, the three of us make our way to the living room to cuddle and watch TV. It's been a great way to relax together after a long day. I am sitting at the end of the sofa, with Raven leaning on me, and River has her head in Raven's lap. It is the absolute best way to end the day; well we could always make it more fun but this is my new happy place,

Like my thoughts made their way into Raven's mind, she takes one hand out of River's hair and starts rubbing it up and down my length. Every time she strokes it through my shorts, I get harder. Since she knows the best way to tease me, she starts squeezing the head every time she passes over it. I try to hold back my groan of pleasure, but I am unsuccessful. River heard me and turned her head to look at us. As soon as she sees what Raven is doing to me, she's working to drive me wild in a totally different way. She has Raven's shirt under her tits with her bra pulled to the side. River takes Raven's right nipple in her mouth

CHAPTER 39

and starts to suck on it while her hand is pinching and playing with the left nipple. It was so hot to watch, I got distracted from Raven working my length.

I whisper in Raven's ear that I want to see her make River come before I take turns in their cunts. I move over to the chair and watch as Raven slowly undresses River between passionate kisses. When she lays River down on the couch, I get the best view of her glistening cunt and the image of her growing belly behind it. Raven kissed down River's body, taking time to worship every inch of her body and place sweet gentle kisses on her belly. When she finally stops teasing her and makes it down to the apex of River's thighs, it's clear that River is coming out of her skin with anticipation.

I watch as Raven licks a long stroke up River's soaking slit. The moans leaving River's mouth, combined with my view, have me aching to take my own length in my hand, but I just want to watch and appreciate the view. After a torturous few minutes where I am loving the sight in front of me, but also jealous, River lets out a moan. It's clear she's close, so Raven keeps her pace just as she's been going. It doesn't take long for River to let out whimper after whimper, her legs shaking. The puddle that is left on our couch, and how soaked Raven's face is, lets us know just how much she enjoyed the attention.

Once River has come down from her high, she tries to stand up, but her legs are still weak. I realize now is my chance to get them where I want them. I guide Raven to sit on the couch, legs spread, before I get River to sit on her knees, spread to either side of Raven's legs. I gently push River's shoulders, getting her to lean over Raven and arch her back. Just as she took Raven's mouth with her own, I pushed my hard length into Raven's tight cunt, causing her to moan loudly, but it was muffled by

River's tongue entering her mouth. I take Raven's cunt with powerful thrusts, and as soon as I can tell she's close, I pull out and push into River. I keep going like this, edging myself and Raven.

Eventually River says this position is hurting her back. So, she lays on the couch and piles pillows under her head, giving her a better angle. She then gets Raven to "sit her beautiful cunt" on her face where I can still pound into Raven. As soon as Raven is straddling River's head, River starts going to town. Licking and sucking Raven's clit, until she has the room full of moans. I take a moment to appreciate the beautiful view in front of me, before I move to stand behind Raven and push in. I can already feel Raven pulsing around me, and now it wont take either of us long to finish. I take Raven's braids in my hand and pull her head back; these women in front of me are everything. I quickly thrust in Raven, trying to time my release with hers. It's not hard and as soon as she's contracting with pleasure around my cock, I fill her pussy with my cum. As I pull out, River starts lapping at Raven's cunt all over again, moaning at our combined taste.

Once we're all happily sticky and satisfied, I lead the three of us up to the shower. I take my time washing them both, my hands gliding over their bodies, worshiping them with my touch. Once I have them all clean, I kneel down under the spray and start talking to River's growing belly. This has become a tradition, Raven and I take turns whispering to our growing belly.

Chapter 40

River

These last few weeks have been spent slowly moving my shit into Raven and Zane's place. The hardest part of the process has been getting my dogs and their cats to get along. It's such a process because my dogs don't really get that they can't play with the cats the same way they play with each other. But I am hopeful that this means they'll do well when the baby gets here.

We come up with some baby names and narrow it down to three; Charlie Rae, Jordan Lee, and Riley Zae. We add an unnecessary amount of stuff to our registry, but it seems like all shit we'll need. But what do I know, this is my first baby. We work with Dakota and Fe to come up with the plan for the baby shower. It is coming so soon.

We ended up having to push the shower back a month, so now I am seven months pregnant. I am huge, I hurt, I'm exhausted, and my migraines and trich are acting up. But today's the day; it's the shower and I decided to actually look nice for a change. I have on a short violet dress that shows off my growing bump. Raven has on a matching teal dress. She helps me do my hair and makeup, giving me a natural glowy look. I feel beautiful for the first time in weeks. I have always struggled with my self image, and as much as Zane and Raven say I'm beautiful, it's hard not to hear his words. Telling me I'm too fat, too this, too that, and as I grow I keep hearing his words.

We finish getting ready just as the first guests officially make it to the house. We spend the first hour snacking, talking, and meeting more friends and family. After an hour, we sit down, open presents, take too many pictures. I cry with every card I open. I feel so loved, so accepted, and welcome. It is such a wonderful feeling. The presents are amazing, special, and thoughtful.

Once the presents are done, Zane calls everyone to come and stand on the deck. He tells everyone we're bringing the dogs out to pick the baby's name. Excited whispers fill the backyard. He goes on to explain that they're all gender neutral names; three different names have been baked inside three dog safe cakes, and whichever dog finishes their cake first will be the name. When all three dogs are brought out, they're on leashes and each of us hold one dog. Fe and Dakota bring the cakes out and place them just outside of the dogs' reach. Once they say go, we lead the dogs forward and let them eat. It is absolutely hilarious and joyous to watch them go to town on these cakes, though I know my dogs and know who will finish first; what I don't know is which name is in his cake. Zane is holding his leash and bent down to pick up the name, yelling out "Charlie Rae" to tears, cheers, and claps.

The rest of the shower passes by quickly and by the end, I am exhausted. I want to stay and help clean up, but I am just too tired. I help carry presents into the nursery and head upstairs to shower and nap.

Once we hit the seven and a half month mark I start having

CHAPTER 40

weekly ultrasounds. I always have someone with me; my mom, Zane, Raven, Fe, Dakota. No one says it, but it's obvious they're worried I might be accosted again. The doctors are checking bubble's position, my vitals, and for preeclampsia. They're so worried about me because of my weight and it makes me mad every time we're at the doctor's office, but we're almost there. We all decide that after I give birth, that I should have an IUD put in and be watched for postpartum. Time feels both slow and fast all at once. Once I hit the end of my eight month of pregnancy and start of the ninth, the Braxton Hicks start and fuck I am not excited for the real deal.

Chapter 41

Zane

River's doctors decide to schedule her to be induced on December 31st, guessing that she'll give birth that night or the next day. We decided to make the most of our first Christmas together as a trio and the last one without a kid. We pulled a name out of a stocking and whose ever name we pulled is whose stocking we filled. We each gave each other a present that was not baby related. It was the perfect laid back Christmas; all the grandparents came and we stayed in matching PJ's all day. It was an amazingly perfect day. I couldn't ask for a better Christmas, surrounded by the people who love me most.

The next few days passed with River home resting and nesting; Raven and I were working as much as possible. We wanted to be sure we were set for when Charlie made their arrival. River was officially waddling around and needed help sitting up, standing up, bending over, all the things. She was exhausted because her body was growing another human, so Raven and I were determined to make her as comfortable as possible,

We got amazing news the day after Christmas; our restraining order had been approved. So, if River's former father-in-law came near her, he'd be arrested again. We were right that he

CHAPTER 41

was let off easy for his first attacks on her. As mad as it made us, we weren't surprised. He was a bitter, wealthy, white man who was well respected in our society. We all knew he was going to get off easy with what he did. The lawyer that had been gifted to us was working overtime to keep River safe though.

Dakota did tell us he had been able to come onto hospital staff full time instead of as needed for his patients, so he was still able to make a good living. We were all nervous about him being at the hospital when River would give birth, but there wasn't a hell of a lot we could do about it. So, we just kept everyone updated and made sure all the medical staff knew the situation and not to let him near her.

When New Year's Eve came you could feel the excitement, anticipation, and nerves rolling off of us. Our hospital bags had been packed, so we were ready to go. Our parents were planning on heading to the hospital shortly after we got there, that way we'd have time to get settled. Once we got to the hospital, I pulled the car up to the drop off and let Raven and River out. River was met with a wheelchair, so she could safely be brought inside. I quickly parked the car and headed in to meet them.

Raven and River had already been taken into a room, so the nurse at the desk led me to room 242. It was a large room, with one bed in the middle. There were several chairs for people to sit in around the room. I am so glad we had our own room and not a shared room. When I walked in, the nurses were taking River's vital signs. Everything looked good, so the nurse headed to get the doctor. The doctor came in and talked us through what was about to happen, before doing a pelvic exam. She confirmed the epidural was wanted, before getting the meds to induce River. Even though she was full term, she wasn't dilated or having contractions. It seemed crazy to me, but apparently

River was three weeks late herself. So, she's not surprised.

River ordered a labor dress, so once everyone leaves the room, I finally get to see her in it. It's a long sleeve emerald green dress that opens in the front and back and ties around the middle. The color of her dress is stunning against her pale skin; it's such a deep color and the contrast has me wanting to draw a portrait of her. I had not brought any of my art things, but I could take photos and surprise her later with a portrait. I leaned over her in the hospital bed, telling her how beautiful she looks, before giving her a kiss. I then walked over to Raven and told her I loved her and kissed her. Our family of three will soon be a family of four.

God, the hospital is fucking boring. I should have brought my art shit. I kinda expected the process to go quickly once she was induced, but that's not the case. They manually broke her water and made it clear that the process could move very quickly or be frustratingly slow. We got here at 8am and we're coming up on the twelve hour mark. Our families came, said hello, and then left to go and buy goods to celebrate the New Year in the hospital. I won't lie, we're all a little worried about the animals tonight, but Fe is staying at the house along with one of his partners. That way if there are any dogs scared by the fireworks, they won't be alone.

When our parents finally make it back to the hospital they have 2025 hats, glasses, plastic champagne flutes, sparkling juice since alcohol isn't an option, and pizzas. We all put on our 2025 gear and start to drink, eat, and celebrate. We have several things to celebrate tonight. Having our family here to celebrate tonight is the bee's knees. We talk, eat, and watch River like hawks in case she goes into labor.

CHAPTER 41

When she was last checked her vitals were normal, her contractions had started and were only a few minutes apart, and she was a couple centimeters dilated. So, our bubble should make their grand entrance within the next few hours. The hours pass in both a blur and slow motion; every time River has a contraction, she squeezes the shit out of either my hand or Raven's. She might have an amazing pain tolerance, but it's clear this is no joke.

When the clock strikes midnight, we all yell, cheer, and celebrate the joy that will fill our year. So, much has changed in the last 9 months. I cannot put into words how glad I am that River barreled into our lives and turned them on their heads. Our parents leave after that, promising to listen for the phones for when Charlie Rae makes their arrival. I am so glad when River is able to get a few hours of sleep, but it's frequently interrupted by nurses and contractions.

When 8am comes around the doctor comes in and tells River it's time to push. Excitement ripples through me; it's time. I am going to be a dad! River is in labor, pushing for hours. I am randomly assaulted by vulgar language and threats to my cock. My cock is hiding from the threats coming his way; the fear of never feeling her wet heat again is very real at this moment. I mean, it is the reason she is cussing in pain and having a human pushed out of her vagina.

After hours of labor, cussing, threats, and nearly broken fingers on my hand, Charlie makes their arrival. Charlie is screaming, making sure we all hear their arrival to this world. They weigh 7.5 pounds and are 19.5 inches long. Both River and Charlie are looked over after the birth; both of their vitals look good! We did request that Charlie not be taken to the nursery, since there are three of us here, we can easily watch her without

River's rest being disturbed too much. This way when Charlie needs to eat, River is already right there and able to whip her boob out. I want to taste the milk so bad, but I feel like it's weird. However, I also know there would be no judgment from River or Raven.

Once the nurses have left and are cleaning Charlie up, I lean down to kiss River's forehead and whisper, "you did so well and I am so in love with you. Thank you for entering my life and turning it upside down." As soon as the words leave my lips, I'm nervous that I said the wrong thing, because tears spring to River's eyes. She's blinking fast, obviously trying to hold them back. Raven walks over, kisses River's forehead and tells her, "I love you too. I am so glad that you completed our trio. I could not ask for better partners." River starts crying harder, unable to get words out, but she holds her hand up with the ASL for "I love you". It is truly the most perfect day.

When the nurse comes in to fill out the birth certificate information, it's bittersweet because we can't all three be listed, since we live in a state where only two parents can be on a birth certificate. Raven was very clear that she was not upset by this fact; she understands and will still be called mom. The title of mom is all that matters to her, and being accepted as mom to everyone in our lives.

We stayed in the hospital for another 24 hours before we're told we could go home. It has been a long couple of days, but everyone got to come and visit us in the hospital and say hi to baby Charlie. Once we got home, it was important to introduce the pets to Charlie in a safe manner, because they're our kids too and aren't going anywhere. They helped us grow and shape us to be great care givers, even if it is on a much smaller table.

CHAPTER 41

Once we got home, I started on a present for Raven and River. I took several photos of them in the hospital, and I hand drew and painted a collage to always remember the day. It's a long rectangular canvas split into three, the middle section being the longest segment. On each of the ends there is an image of each of them alone; Raven has a huge smile on her face and River is laughing. The middle drawing is of them together, foreheads touching as they both look down on the little miracle in River's arms. On the back I title it, "Mama and Mom, 1/1/2025".

The painting took me a few months to do, especially since I had to hide that I was doing it. But it was important to me that I got it right and they had no idea about it. One day when they were both out, I hung the canvas up on the living room wall for all to see. It was an agonizing few hours waiting for them to get home. I spent most of those hours pacing the room and second guessing the placement, but I knew in my heart of hearts it was in the perfect spot.

When they finally make it home, I meet them at the door like an eager puppy. Charlie is with River's parents for the night to give us a night off, so it's just the three of us. I ask them to both close their eyes, take both of their hands, and lead them to the living room. They won't stop asking what's going on and probing for answers, but I kept my lips sealed. When we were all in the living room, standing in front of the drawing I told them they could open their eyes. Their jaws literally dropped, and they looked absolutely stunned. They kept opening and closing their mouths like fish, unsure what to say. I am nervously standing there, just waiting for their approval, because God damn do I need it. Suddenly River pulls my head to face her and she kisses me, hard. When she pulls away she whispers, "it is beautiful. I had no idea I needed this but now that I do it's obvious." Next Raven pulls my head to face her, branding my lips with hers whispering "it's perfect. You're amazing. We love you."

Before I know what's happening, River is down on her knees in front of me, looking up at me through her lashes as she pulls down my sweat pants. I gasp as she takes my length into her mouth, but Raven kisses me, cutting my gasp short. River works my length with expertise, sucking hard on the head before taking me to the back of her throat and gagging, while one of her hands cups and caresses my balls.

Once she has me on the edge of coming, she pulls away and leads Raven to the couch. They kiss and strip as they walk, leaving a trail of clothes behind them. Once they're naked and making out in front of the couch, River guides Raven to lay down and spread her legs. Raven's top half is laying back against the couch, her right leg is lined up with the back of the couch, and her left leg bent on the floor. Her pussy is on full display for us. River gets on her knees before Raven, licking and kissing all over her body, before she takes a long lick of her center. With the way River is bent over, her pussy is just asking to be taken, so I do just that; guiding my length to her entrance and taking her brutally. Our fuck fest is hard, fast, and sweaty. Raven comes first as River sucks hard on her clit. I pound harder into River, knowing she needs a mouth or a toy to come. I groan as I empty into her, then I flip her over and start eating her cunt; it tastes of our mixed juices. Raven and River are making out as I suck on River's clit; it's not long before she's coming too.

I couldn't ask for a better life.

CHAPTER 41

Dear Reader,

Thank you for joining me on this journey. This is my debut romance book and it holds a special place in my heart. I don't read many books with widows and as I am a widow, I felt like it was a great first book for me to write. While some aspects of this story mimic my life, a lot do not. I have a great relationship with my late husband's parents for one and I do not have any kids. I hope this story speaks to you, like it did for me. I hope you find all of the love and acceptance you're looking for. I hope to continue to write romance books of all kinds. I aim to show accurate representation, so please email me,authorlavendernicole@gmail.com, if there is something that does not feel authentic or appropriate to you. In addition, If there is a grammar or spelling error please email me instead of reporting it to kindle. I truly hope you enjoyed this book, it is near and dear to my heart. My friend drew the art for the cover and it is *chefs kiss*, but he does not want his name attached to it since he is not part of the romance book world.

Thanks,
Lavender Nicole

Acknowledgments

I want to thank my family and friends for being their to support me on this journey. My friend who did my cover art but who does not want to be named, thank you. Alyssa Huck who helped alpha read and edit Tattooed on Their Hearts. My wonderful bookish friends, including Kenzie Young and H.A. Wills who are authors that supported me and advised me in this journey. My wonderful PA Cheyanne Cruz. And finally all my wonderful readers. I love each and everyone of you.

About the Author

Hello beautiful people,

   Lavender Nicole is a plus size widow who started writing this book to feature widows getting a second chance at love. Lavender also has chronic illnesses, which she wanted to represent in her books. Lavender is also part of the LGBTQIA+ community. When she isn't working or writing she can be found at home with her dogs, Ginny, Schnapps, and Scotch, listening to audio books, watching falcons football, or GMM/Try Guys on youtube. She is also on youtube herself reviewing books in the most chaotic way with her friend, Crimson. Lavender has been finding herself and the most important things in her life since witnessing her husband end his own life.

You can connect with me on:
◼ https://www.facebook.com/authorlavendernicole
🔗 https://www.tiktok.com/@lifewithdogsandaudiobooks?_t=8rm7YKuqCN9&_r=1
🔗 https://www.instagram.com/authorlavendernicole/profilecard/?igsh=dmY30GNxZzQ5dnc5

www.ingramcontent.com/pod-product-compliance
Lightning Source LLC
LaVergne TN
LVHW041709070526
838199LV00045B/1274